A Dope Boys' Seduction 3

Tina J

Copyright 2018

More Books by Tina J

A Thin Line Between Me & My Thug 1-2
I Got Luv for My Shawty 1-2
Kharis and Caleb: A Different kind of Love 1-2
Loving You is a Battle 1-3
Violet and the Connect 1-3
You Complete Me
Love Will Lead You Back
This Thing Called Love
Are We in This Together 1-3
Shawty Down to Ride For a Boss 1-3
When a Boss Falls in Love 1-3
Let Me Be The One 1-2
We Got That Forever Love
Ain't No Savage Like The One I got 1-2
A Queen & Hustla 1-3 (collab)
Thirsty for a Bad Boy 1-2
Hasaan and Serena: An Unforgettable Love 1-2
We Both End Up With Scars
Caught up Luvin a beast 1-3
A Street King & his Shawty 1-2
I Fell for the Wrong Bad Boy 1-2 (collab)
Addicted to Loving a Boss 1-3
All Eyes on the Crown 1-3
I Need that Gangsta Love 1-2 (collab)
Still Luvin' a Beast 1-2
Creepin' With The Plug 1-2
I Wanna Love You 1-2
Her Man, His Savage 1-2
When She's Bad, I'm Badder 1-3
Marco & Rakia 1-3
Feenin' for a Real One 1-3
A Kingpin's Dynasty 1-3
What Kind Of Love Is This?
Frankie & Lexi 1-3
A Dope Boy's Seduction 1-3

Previously…

"You sure about this bro?" I asked my twin as we sat in the house packing things up to move. Zia, said she may have decided to come live with him but she refused to stay in a place he spent years in with another woman.

"I'm killing everyone to bring these mothafucka's to the forefront. Tariq is on the run, Riley is MIA and Jordan, I'm sure is plotting somewhere."

"Babe, do you need this?" Zia came out the kitchen with some pots and pans.

"Are you using them to cook for me?"

"Yea fucking right? I wish, I would use some of the same shit she did. You said you're getting a new house, therefore; everything in it should be knew."

"Then why you ask him?"

"Fazza, you're on my shit list after cheating on my friend so I'd stay outta it."

5

"Yea, yea. Did she tell you how she came by when you were attacked and tried to fuck first? Some friend she is?" Zia stood there with her mouth open.

"You ain't shit." Maz said.

"She did. Y'all both know she missed my ass." Zia sucked her teeth and left us in the living room.

"Anyway, when you wanna do it?"

"Whenever. I wanna make sure she's safe at moms first."

"Moms?" I questioned.

"Bro, they haven't even met."

"I know but they've spoken on the phone and ma knows what's up."

"Oh. I was about to say, you bugging."

"Mazza, I'm ready. We been here all morning and I'm hungry, tired and.-"

"Horny right? You wanna fuck my brother into a coma, right?"

"I was gonna say sleepy. What is wrong with you? Mazza, is he always a pervert?"

"All his life. We can go though. I'm hungry too." He stood and walked over to her.

I dropped the tape and went to grab my phone off the table. I opened the photo and it was Ty naked in the house. I had to grab my self because she was at work right now, and I know she was being funny. Little does she know. I'll snatch her ass right outta there and fuck her in the bathroom.

"I know you want me to meet your mom, but can we go tomorrow? I wanna be rested up." She whispered something in his ear and he grinned.

"Told you she wanted to fuck." I shook my head.

"Actually, I just wanna suck him off."

"Oh shit Maz. You got a freak?"

"By Fazza. It's never a pleasure." She stuck her tongue out and told Mazza, she'd meet him in the car. He watched her walk out. Yea, this nigga in love.

"The movers will be here in the morning. We out." Mazza said and I followed them out the door. *Goodbye Riley*, I whispered to myself. A nigga was happy as hell she was no longer in my brother's life.

7

****

"What are you doing here?" The bitch said in a nasty tone. I couldn't stand her either. Pops never said much, but too bad he's gonna suffer too.

"Move your old ass out the way." I pushed Riley's mom to the side and went in the kitchen. I smelled food cooking and a nigga was hungry. I went in the kitchen and there was some sort of stew simming in the pot.

"Where's your daughter?" I heard my brother ask.

"I wouldn't tell you where she was, even if you had a gun to my head."

CLICK! I didn't have to look, to know he had one pointed at her.

"What were you saying?"

"Please don't kill me." I heard her begging and went in to see her crying with her hands up.

"Funny how your tone changed." I said and laughed.

"Where is she?"

"In Maryland with a new guy." Mazza nodded and stood behind her.

"Call your husband in here." She did like he asked and the look on his face was priceless. He had no idea what was going on.

"Kill him." Mazza said and placed the gun in her hand.

"What?"

"Kill him." Her father was nervous as fuck.

"You boss him around, treat him like shit and who knows what else. You may as well get rid of him because you don't appreciate him."

"I won't kill my husband."

"Fine!"

BOOM! BOOM!

"Oh my God!" She dropped to her knees.

"Your turn." She looked at Mazza.

"Why are you doing this?"

"You never liked me or approved of our relationship anyway, so why does it matter?"

"You're just like that other man." Mazza placed the gun on her head.

"What man?" Her mom had a sneaky grin on her face.

"The same man who mentored you, is the same man Riley..." She stopped.

"How do you know Shakim?"

"Maybe you should ask my daughter."

"I will." Mazza shot straight through her skull.

"What did she mean by our mentor is the same man? How did Riley know him?" He asked pacing the floor.

"Bro, I don't know. Let's get this shit cleaned up and head out to Maryland to find the bitch." This time he didn't ask me not to call her that and agreed to leave ASAP. After everything was done at Riley's parents' house we walked to our cars.

"I'll be over when I drop this lunch off to Ty." I told Maz and hopped in my car to run to Quik Chek. When I got to the hospital, I parked and went to the front door, only to be stopped by two officers I've never seen before.

"Are you Fazza Chambers?" One of them asked.

10

"I'm not sure. I have amnesia sometimes." I gave him a fake smile and tried to go in the building.

"Do you have ID on you?"

"Didn't I just tell your punk ass, I have amnesia? Tha fuck. You don't listen well."

"That's him officer." I turned around and saw this bitch standing there with her arms folded and a grin on her face.

"Word! You called the cops?"

"Yup!" The other officer took the food out my hand and asked me to place my hands behind my back.

"What is going on?" Ty ran over to me.

"Take these cuffs off of him." She pushed the cop.

"Ty, stop. You're pregnant. I'll be fine."

"Fazza, you didn't do anything. What is going on?" I looked over at the woman standing there grinning.

"This bitch called the cops on me." Ty turned to look.

"You're going to jail." She screamed out as the officers read me my rights. That bitch better find her black dress right now because I promise, she's dying.

"When did Tionne wake up?" I asked Shawn who was standing out the door.

"About an hour ago." I could tell he shed some tears by how red his eyes were.

"About damn time." We exchanged hugs and I stepped in to find Shakim junior, her daughter, my mom, aunt and I was introduced to Shawn's parents.

"Mazza, oh my God." She said barely above a whisper and reached out for me to hug her.

"Tha fuck? You engaged?" I asked looking down on her finger. The ring wasn't there yesterday and I would've noticed because the rock was huge.

"He asked, the minute I opened my eyes. You're not mad, are you?"

"Not at all. He's a good dude cuz and I just want what's best for you." I kissed her cheek and stood there as she asked everyone to give us a moment. I'm not sure what she wanted to discuss but whatever it is, sounded serious.

"Is the door closed?" I looked and told her yes.

12

"Can you pass me some water?" I handed it to her and told her, if she wanted to wait to speak she could but she insisted.

"Mazza, what I'm about to tell you may hurt a little but I need you to understand, I didn't tell you because I had to be sure."

"What are you talking about Tionne?"

"Remember when you asked why I didn't like Riley?"

"Yea."

"Well the reason I came by that night was to tell you she had something to do with Shakim's death." It was like the wind was knocked outta me.

"Tell me you just made that shit up."

"Mazza, her and Shakim used to…"

"WHERE'S MAZZA! MAZZA!" I heard what sounded like Ty screaming outside the door and ran to open it.

"What's wrong?" She was shaking and crying.

"You have to get him." I grabbed her arms.

"Get who? Ty, what's wrong? Is it my brother?" She nodded her head yes.

"What happened?" My entire family and Shawn was standing there waiting on her to speak.

"I went to get my lunch from him and he was being arrested."

"ARRESTED!" Everyone shouted.

"Yes. She had him arrested."

"Who? Who had him arrested? Ty, calm down." Her body was shaking harder and not even ten seconds later, she passed out. Shawn caught her right before her head hit the ground. All the nurses came running over.

"What the hell is going on? Mazza, go get your brother." My mom said.

"I'm coming." Shawn said and both of us stood to leave.

"Its about time we meet up again." I looked up and this nigga was standing there with a machine gun. I had to laugh because his unsteady ass was shaking.

"This is about to go left Shawn. Get the family inside the room." It took him a minute to leave but I heard him behind me telling everyone to get in rooms ad close the door. People were yelling and screaming.

14

"Lets' get this shit over with." He smiled and so did I.

This was going to be an easy kill.

"You sure you wanna do this?" I asked moving closer. Tariq may have worked for us all these years, but he really had no clue how bad he fucked up.

"You didn't have to kill her?" I shook my head at how dumb he sounded. Nigga's always wanna know why you murdered someone close to them for their shit. Like we're supposed to excuse all the bullshit they did or said.

"Says the man who sliced my girl down the arm and tried to take her hand off." I continued moving closer and he hadn't moved an inch. I don't know if he's really stupid or so frozen with fear, he couldn't.

"You know Tariq, I really thought this was over what happened to your brother, but I should've known better. You are one selfish ass nigga."

"Fuck him. He shouldn't have stolen from those old people."

"Are you kidding me right now? Your family didn't have shit and you were parading yourself out on the streets like some big timer while your family was suffering."

16

"Well, you and your brother took care of that, now didn't you?" He smirked and lifted the gun.

"We shouldn't have had to because that's not our family. Tariq you could've taken care of them and still had tons of money left over." He stood there looking stupid and completely ignored my statement.

"Why did you kill her? My son won't have a mother and…"

"We left you alone, even after Fazza beat your ass but you kept trying us and it is, what it is at this point."

"I don't know how to raise a kid."

"Actually, your mother will take care of your kid because you're about to die." He had the nerve to look shocked.

"You want this bullet in your head or gut?" I asked removing my weapon outta my waist and pointed it at him.

"You're gonna die first." He said and I wasn't even worried.

"WAIT!" I yelled out.

"How did you find out about Zia?" He smirked. It probably wasn't the right time to ask because the cops would be here soon but I had to know.

"I was gonna kill Riley but after she gave me the pussy and told me how she found out about some bitch in Maryland, I changed my mind. Yo, she had some of the best pussy I ever had." I turned my face up. I never would've guessed Riley was not only grimy but she was giving pussy away like candy too.

"Enough said." I wanted to make sure the story his baby mama gave me and his matched before taking his life. Some may ask why I didn't just kill him on sight. I liked fucking with people before they die. It's like the anticipation of knowing they're about to die gives me an adrenaline rush.

I stared at this stupid motherfucker with the gun and let a grin cross my face. Not only was he scared, nervous and looked like shit; he had no idea how to handle the type of artillery in his hand. He was shaking, paranoid as hell and most of all, in a fucked-up situation. If you come for someone, make sure you know how to handle your weapon of choice.

I wanted to laugh but then again, he had everyone in here frantic and the only way to keep them calm, is to de-escalate the situation. I had my finger on the trigger and was just about to pull it.

TAT! TAT! Tariq's body hit the floor, yet he wasn't dead. I turned to see Shawn putting his gun away.

"I couldn't allow you to shoot him with all these people watching."

"I don't give a fuck about that."

PHEW! PHEW! I let two shots off in his head and put my gun away. I understand where Shawn coming from but ain't no way in hell, I'm letting them haul Tariq's ass away to be saved. What if he survives and starts talking? I'm not about to fuck up what we built for a trifling ass nigga.

"I know you don't but your family needs you." I turned to see my mom, cousins, his parents and a bunch of others peeking out the doors. So much for staying in the room.

"I'm going to have this cleaned up. Is your gun registered?"

"This one is." I gave him a fake smile.

19

"Ok. They're going to check the surveillance video and most likely call you down. Even though you were defending yourself, they'll still wanna check." I nodded. All of a sudden, cops came swarming in from all the exits.

"Get outta here Mazza." My mom yelled.

"Ma."

"GO!" She pushed me in the opposite direction. I looked on the ground at Tariq, then over at my mom.

"Tell Shawn, I'll call him later." She kissed my cheek and told me to check on my brother.

"Yo! Where is Ty?" I asked one of the nurses who was staring at everything going on.

"Ty?" She questioned with a confused look.

"The nurse who passed out. Where is she?"

"Oh, on the floor upstairs. Someone said she was pregnant, so they placed her on the labor and delivery floor."

"FUCK! Ok thanks." I ran up the steps and pressed the button on the floor. The doors opened, I asked where Ty's room was and walked down there. I went inside and she had monitors on and there were some beeping noises.

"Ty?" She rolled over and you could see how puffy her eyes were.

"Is Fazza ok? Please don't tell me he cut up and the cops shot him or something. You know they think they're above the law." She asked and sat up. The machine started beeping.

"I don't know yet but you have to relax."

"I'm trying to but…"

"There is no but. You know he's gonna be fine. As far as you go, I'd get it together because we both know if anything happens to the baby, Fazza isn't going to take it well. I'm not saying he'll kill you but I think we both know something bad will happen." She started laughing.

"The crazy thing is, I think Fazza loves the baby more than me now." She wiped her nose, with her hand. I handed her a tissue.

"Ty, all I can say is, my brother is very much in love with you and the baby. I've never in my life witnessed him become obsessed over one woman and trust me, he's had a lot."

"Spare me Mazza."

"I'm just saying. He may have loved Shanta but not the way he loves you. I think it's because you don't take his shit, y'all have fun together and he knows you have his back no matter what."

"I do Mazza and I'm very much in love with him too. He hurt me but I honestly believe he won't do it again."

"Shit, he better not. He got on all our nerves waiting on you to take him back."

"Yea well his ass better learn from it because that's the only pass he'll get."

"I'm gonna let you say that because I don't think he'll cheat again, but you do know you're stuck with him for life?" She sucked her teeth.

"I see you're good so I'm gonna go find out what's going on with him." I kissed her cheek and was almost at the door when she called out for me.

"Mazza, please don't let him kill her."

"Kill who?"

"Kill the person who had him arrested."

"I'm not sure I can stop him. My brother may have his fucked-up ways about him but once it's in his head to get at someone, no one can stop him."

"I may not care for her, but I don't want him taken away from me either for murder." I walked back to her on the bed.

"Who is it?" She blew her breath out and fell on the pillow behind her.

"My mother."

"Oh shit, you know I can't stop that. He's been itching to kill her for a minute now and hasn't because of you."

"I know."

"I'll try Ty but there's no promises coming from me." I went to leave again and this time she didn't stop me. I don't know what she thought would happen and I will talk to Faz but we all know, he's not going to let her off the hook. Ty, better bid her farewells now.

****

"What up? What they saying?" I asked Shawn who beat me to the station. I called the lawyer when I was on my way to see Ty, and I'm sure he's been here already if not still here.

"Not much. She's here tryna keep him behind bars." He pointed to Ty's mom who was sitting in one of the chairs speaking to an officer.

"Why you look stressed?" He ran his hand down his face.

"Unfortunately, I'm the one who took the call that day and she's saying I saw everything."

"Did you?" He pulled me into one of the corners.

"No, but he did threaten her." He whispered to make sure no one heard him.

"What actually happened?'

"I can't even tell you."

"So how is she saying you saw everything, if you didn't?"

"Exactly!" We both looked in her direction and her mouth was running a mile, a minute.

"When I got there, he was standing and she was on the floor. She started talking shit and you know how your brother gets. He said some off the wall shit and left. Man, that was weeks ago and really, she doesn't have a leg to stand on but they had to bring him in because she made it seem like it happened yesterday. Do you know the bitch got a receipt from the door people saying it was kicked off the hinges and not broken, to prove he came to her house and entered it aggressively?"

"Will it stand though?"

"No because I went over the video footage that day and it showed him coming there but the camera wasn't angled correctly so you didn't see him kick the door off."

"I'm lost then. How can they bring him in?"

"She fears for her life."

"As she should." I said not sugar-coating shit.

"I know but as hard as its going to be, we have to keep him away from her for now. Whatever he does after the judge sees him, he can do what he wants." I nodded and waited for them to bring him out. His bail was only 5k and our lawyer was getting that back because he said she waited too long to press charges and its clear she wants to cause friction in his relationship. It's too bad she won't be around to see her grandchild born but this is what happens when you fuck with the Chamber twins.

"You think he's gonna kill her?" I asked Ms. Chambers who came in to check on me. The doctors were making me stay for a few hours for observation.

"Do you want my honest answer, or the one you'd rather hear to keep your sanity?" She asked and sat next to me on the bed.

"I'm not sure either will suffice at this point." She took my hand in hers and wiped the tears off my face.

"Ty, you've come to love my son and everyone knows he feels the same. What you may not have realized is he isn't dealing with a full deck." She started laughing.

"I'm not talking about being mentally ill or anything like that, I'm talking about a man who is above the law and doesn't give a shit about facing consequences for his actions."

"But…"

"If it were Mazza, he may not do it because he's the calmer one but if Fazza has it in his head, you can forget it."

"I don't know what to do because my dad passed away and she's the only one I have left."

"Ty, I understand and I'm sure it's the exact reason he hasn't dealt with her sooner but ask yourself this." She scooted closer.

"What happens if he doesn't touch her and she continues to harass him? What if she does stupid shit to provoke him? What if when the baby comes, she does something drastic to hurt him? Or what happens when you wanna have something at your house and can't invite her?" I sat there listening to every word she said.

"She's your mother Ty and I can't imagine trying to make a decision like you but there are consequences for what she did and Fazza isn't going to let it fly. Do you honestly think your mother is going to stop coming for him?" I couldn't answer because we both know the truth.

"She hates him Ty and a person filled with that much hate, won't be able to get over it." I nodded because she was right. My mom despised him and the feeling is mutual.

"She's my mother and he's my man, slash baby father. I want both of them in my life and if not, I don't want either of them dead. How do I make a decision like that?"

28

"At this point Ty, you don't have to because your mother made the decision for you."

"Huh?"

"Your mother knows the type of man Fazza is and still came for him. She also knows you're in love and have a child on the way." I understood but I still don't want him in jail or my mother dead.

"Listen." She stood and went to grab the phone that was ringing in her purse.

"As a mother, all we want is what's best for our children and with that, our kids may have people enter their lives we may not like. However; it doesn't give us the right to try and destroy anything." I sat quiet.

"I would think she was doing it out of the love she has for you, but your mother is being spiteful, hateful and most of all, letting the anger get the best of her." She looked at the phone and put it back down.

"If she really loved you, none of this would be happening."

"I know."

"She'd be watching from a distance and being the shoulder to cry on if need be. You know this Ty."

"I do go to her sometimes."

"You may but only for certain things." She stared at me and spoke again.

"Ty, you didn't even tell her Fazza cheated on you because you knew in your heart, she'd judge, criticize and try to get you to leave him. You didn't wanna hear it, which is exactly why you kept it to yourself."

"I love my mom and I don't want her to die because of who I chose."

"Its outta our hands Ty." I didn't say anything, pulled the covers up and laid on my side. She took that as me saying I needed time alone and I can't say she's wrong. I needed time to regroup and figure out how I can be with a man who's going to make me prepare a funeral for my mother.

****

Two hours went by and the doctor came in and said he was discharging me. I was a little upset Fazza hadn't come to see me, but then again, I have no idea what's going on down at

30

the jail. Mazza, did let me know he was there and they would be letting him out soon. He also mentioned my mother, trying her hardest to keep him in there.

I know my mom has her evil ways but why is she going this hard for Fazza? Is she really that mad he shot me? I feel like Ms. Chambers; if I can move on from it, why can't she? Does she not want me to be happy? Whatever the case, I'm going to get to the bottom of it.

I began putting my clothes on when the nurse walked in with the discharge papers. I was so stressed out after seeing Fazza get locked up and finding out my mom is responsible, that I passed out. I didn't hit the ground but all my vitals were high and they had me stay to make sure everything was good. I didn't expect to stay as long as I did, but you can never be too careful. If anything was wrong, I was in the right place.

I signed the papers, gathered my things and headed out. The nurses all spoke and told me to take care. Most of the employees here are pretty cool with me, so I appreciated the well wishes. Some jobs have a lot of cattiness going and it definitely goes on here but when you stay in your lane, you tend not to get caught up in any of it.

I went to the parking garage, unlocked my door and drove home. I thought about stopping by my mothers to confront her but after talking to Fazza's mom and thinking about what all happened, it's in my best interest to wait. I didn't wanna risk losing this child and Fazza kill me. I know for a fact my mother would say something stupid to make me stress on purpose.

As much as she doesn't want me to have this child, is as much as I want it. I'm not saying the baby is to spite her because I was fully aware of him squirting in me. However, after seeing the ultrasound and attending the first appointment, I was already in love with my child.

Fazza and I prepared for this child and my mother is taking away all the joy in being pregnant and for what; her hatred towards him? I have to see her soon and find out what the hell is going on in her head, otherwise; I'm gonna stress myself out regardless.

I went in the house and stripped to wash myself up, today, was stressful and interesting to say the least.

"Hey." I spoke when he entered in the shower behind me. I heard him come in the house and continued about my business. When he's ready to speak, he will. That's just how he is.

"You look sexy as hell pregnant." He turned me around to face him.

"And you are sexy altogether."

"I am right." I had to laugh. I let both of my hands slide up his chest and wrap around his neck.

"I tell these ho's all the time, this sexy motherfucka is off the market. If they want me, they have to fantasize."

"I don't want them doing that either. Any fantasies, memories and banging ass sex belong to me."

"Oh yea." His hands gripped my ass.

"Yup. Unless you leaving me alone."

"Never gonna happen Ty." He lifted me up in his arms and I let my head rest on his shoulder.

"Stop stressing before you end up back in the hospital and I really have to kill you." I pinched the side of his cheek.

"I'm serious Ty. I don't want you worrying about today or any day after. Leave all your worries with me."

"How am I supposed to do THATTTTTTTT!" I screamed out when he initiated making us one.

"You feel so damn good Ty. That month was long as hell, don't do that again." He slammed me down harder and I arched my back as the massive orgasm took over.

"I won't baby. Fuck, I won't."

"Good, now fuck me back." I popped up and down the way he wanted and the two of us ended up having more sex in the bedroom, on the floor and in the kitchen when we tried to eat. He was making up for lost time so he says. I swore we did already but I guess not in his eyes.

"I'm not going to tell you when, but it's going to happen." Fazza said and stood up to get dressed.

"Where are you going?"

"Oh, I'm getting ready for you to kick me out."

"I didn't.-"

"You don't have to say it now but by the time this conversation is over, I'll be dressed and escorting my own self out."

"Do you have to kill her?"

"Ty, let me be clear in case you don't understand what's really going on." He threw his jeans on.

"Your mother is a bitch and we all know this." I nodded my head.

"She's disliked me from the very beginning and that's fine because I'm not here for everyone to approve of me. However, your mother is trying to put me in jail and I'm not talking about for kicking her door off the hinges."

"I had no idea that even happened."

"I know because I keep things away from you, and the reason she never mentioned it to you is because she already concocted a plan in her head as to what she would do."

"She's harmless Fazza."

"I was arrested Ty, on some shit that took place weeks ago. I don't even know how the shit is possible but its whatever." He sat to put his sneakers on. I could tell he was trying to calm himself down.

"You want everything to be ok but it's not that easy."

"Fazza, let me talk to her."

"Just forget it Ty. I don't want you bringing anything up and she turn on you."

"She's mad right now Fazza and.-" He stood in front of me and smiled. I could tell he was getting aggravated but I still wanted my mom to be around for a long time. If talking is getting through to him, then so be it.

"I get it baby, I do but she made her bed and a fatal consequence awaits her. I'm sorry."

"You're going to end her life because she said you kicked the door off the hinges?" He swung around with that same evil look on his face, the time I smacked him. I was scared but not too scared because this time it wasn't over me.

"TY, SHE SAID, I TRIED TO FUCKING RAPE HER." My mouth hit the floor. It felt like my body was on fire and a migraine was coming on. I began to hyperventilate and my air supply seemed to disappear. There's no way my mother would say he tried to rape her. I couldn't move from my spot on the bed and the tears were now blinding me.

"Calm the fuck down Ty." He came over with a wet rag and wiped my face.

"I… I… I…. can't. Why did she… say that?" I was stuttering and trying to catch my breath all at once.

"Fuck this." I heard and Fazza got up off the bed. I felt him lifting my arms to put a shirt on, then laid me back to put some leggings on. It's like, I was in a state of shock and couldn't move. He lifted my body, took me down the steps and placed me in the car. We didn't drive far and all I remember was hearing his mom ask what happened and a door close. *Did I just die?*

I stared over at my girl in the passenger seat, as she tried to keep herself calm after hearing what her mother accused me of. I didn't wanna tell her but she repeatedly asked me not to kill the bitch. Unfortunately, even if I had a second to renege on murdering her, it went straight out the window the minute she falsely accused me of trying to rape her old ass. What the hell would I even get outta touching her? *Yuk!* I thought to myself as I drove to my mothers.

Seeing my girl hyperventilate, scared the shit outta me and instead of taking her back to the hospital, I'm dropping her off to my mother to handle some things. The two of them speak a lot and I know nothing will happen here.

The crazy part about this entire ordeal is, I truly believe Ty's mother is lonely and wants her daughter to live with her. She has no life and feels like I took her away, which I understand but damn the lengths she's going through is beyond ridiculous, and I'm gonna have fun getting rid of her.

I pulled up at my mothers, carried Ty in and into one of the bedrooms. She was calm now and I told her to try and sleep.

She asked where I was going and I told her, downstairs to talk to my mom. If she knew I was leaving, she'd probably try to go with me and that's not happening.

"I see she didn't take it well." My mom said after I came out the room.

"I wasn't tryna tell her ma, but she kept trying to save her mom and I get it but she took it too far. I'm not about to do time for some bullshit." She sat next to me.

"Are you sure this is what you wanna do?" I let the palm of my hand rub over the top of my head.

"Ma, I know her mother is all she has but the repercussions of attempted rape could land me in jail for at least ten years. I'm not about to let my kid visit me locked up over some bullshit." She nodded her head.

"Do you know her lawyer is trying to throw the book at me on some other bogus ass charges?"

"What you mean?"

"She's saying I tried to rape her, choked her, dragged her down the hall and some other nonsense. She is really reaching."

"They know you didn't do it." I could tell how disgusted she was.

"They know ma, but this is the same lawyer who has been trying to take me and Maz down since Shakim passed."

"Are you serious?"

"Yes."

"Don't they know that's a conflict of interest?"

"It's the same thing my lawyer said and right now, it's only hearsay and there's not much to go off on."

"The bitch is crazy." I laughed at my mom's because she only met Ty's mom once and it wasn't a good introduction.

"It doesn't mean she didn't say other shit. I mean, how can they even pursue me without some sort of evidence?"

"They don't have any." She said.

"Exactly! The only thing I can think of is she is working with someone to make up false accusations. Hell, I didn't even beat the bitch ass like I wanted to so there's no visual marks or anything."

"What the fuck you looking at?" I asked the bitch when I was leaving the jail.

"A man who's going away for a very long time." She smiled as she said it.

"Wait on it." I flashed a smirk in her direction.

"Officer, make sure you write down that he attempted to rape me." I stopped and so did my brother and lawyer. What the hell did she mean attempted rape?

"Excuse me!" My lawyer, myself and Mazza looked at her.

"Your client tried to rape me at my home and he must go to jail." My lawyer glanced over at me and I gave him the yea fucking right look.

"Ma'am that's a serious allegation and if that is the case, why are you just now mentioning it?"

"Do you know who he is? I'm scared for my life and you are allowing him to walk outta here."

"Bitch, you'll need to be scared after this." I tried to beat her ass but my brother and a few officers had to hold me back.

"Do you see how he's acting? How can I feel safe with someone like this roaming the streets?" She was milking the

hell outta her dumb ass lawyer, who had a smile on his face.

The officers knew she was lying but none of them said a word.

They knew she was a dead woman walking.

"Calm down Faz." My brother whispered in my ear.

"You need to control your client or he'll be under the
cell until court." My lawyer had a grin on his face.

"You know better than that." My lawyer was in his face
now.

"However, I will say that if your client here is lying,
not only will she be brought up on charges for filing a false
police report; I'll make up a ton of other charges to make sure
she never sees her freedom again." My lawyer smiled at Ty's
mom who looked shook.

"So, I suggest you have a long talk with your client
because we both know, you're not going to win trying to bet
against me. Let's go Mr. Chambers."

"I'm going to kill you." I mouthed and fear plagued
her face.

"Oh my God! Did you see that? He just threatened
me." She started asking for them to look over the cameras and

to place her in the witness protection plan. When I say she was

doing too much, she really was. We walked out the precinct

and made plans to meet up later in the week to discuss the case.

"Fazza, you ok?" My mom broke me outta my thoughts.

"Yea, I was just thinking about how dumb Ty's mom

looked in the jail. Can you believe she's going this far to keep

me from her?"

"I can because she's evil and evil people do crazy

things."

"Well guess who messed around and met someone ten

times worse?" I smiled and stood to leave.

"I'll be back later. Do you mind if she stays?"

"Of course not."

"Whatever you do, don't let her leave. I don't need her

trying to see her mom."

"She's good but you be careful." I leaned down and

kissed her cheek.

"Always."

****

"You sure about this?" Kelly asked and tossed the cocktail in the window. How he gonna ask me if I'm sure and throw the shit before I answer?

"Positive." We waited until the flames kicked in and ran back to the car, that was parked down the street.

Not too long after, Ty's mom came running out the house in her pajamas. You could see the frantic look on her face through the binoculars I had. People came rushing out their homes as the fire began to burn outta control. The cocktail Kelly threw inside didn't have any of our fingerprints on it and by the time anyone gets here, it will be destroyed as well.

I wasn't worried about the video footage because the tech guy we have, tapped into the system. The security guy watching would never know anything happened because the cameras showed the same shit over and over, which is nothing.

About five minutes later, firetrucks could be heard in the distance but the house was damn near destroyed by now. Someone must've called and that's when you noticed the security guy come running out looking completely lost.

People think Mazza is the calmer one and it may be true but right now, I think I'm the one. I clearly could've barged in the house and killed her but nope. I'm going to make her paranoid. She'll never know when I'll hit and I wanna keep it that way.

"What you think Ty is gonna say?" I had Kelly pull off and head in the direction back to my mom's.

"At this point, she won't say anything because her mom is still breathing. She'll have a lot to say when it's time for her to identify the body."

"Then what?"

"Then, on the way to her mom's funeral, I'll fuck the shit outta her in the back and she'll be stress free inside." Kelly busted out laughing but I was dead ass serious.

Ty is definitely gonna be mad but she also knew the type of nigga I was prior to meeting me. Ain't nothing change because I'm dicking her down and put a baby in her. I'm still the same nigga and will remain that way. She better get used to it because she ain't going nowhere.

"You ignorant as fuck!"

"You already know." We slapped hands and I opened the car door to get out at my mom's.

"See ya." I waved, unlocked the door and went inside. My mom was talking on the phone as she laid on the couch. She looked at me and pointed upstairs. I mouthed the words *goodnight* and went to lay up.

I opened the door and Ty was knocked out, with her mouth open and hair all over the place. I undressed, took a quick shower, dried off and hopped in the bed. I moved some hair out her face and pecked her lips. I stared and mentally prepared myself for all the drama that's going to happen with her mother. But the fact still remains, that Ty ain't going nowhere and I mean that shit.

"Why are you calling me Jordan?" I answered walking down the steps of the house Mazza brought me. Unfortunately, after the guy stabbed me, Mazza refused to let me stay here or anywhere for that matter, where he's not at.

"What you mean, why am I calling you? Ever since that hoodlum boyfriend of your moms hit me with his gun and you left me at the altar per say, I've been trying to get in touch with you. Then, I show up at your job and they say someone tried to kill you. Last but not least, I come to check on you at the hospital and get attacked by that thug guy."

"You mean the thug guy you were about to do business with!" I laughed at his ignorance.

"Yea well, that didn't work out and it was best because it looks like you spread your legs to the highest bidder."

"What the fuck did you say?" I was beyond pissed at this point.

"You heard me. We were supposed to be getting married and having our own family. Who knew you'd go out being a ho?"

47

"First of all, motherfucker. You treated me like shit for years and once you realized I was really leaving, all of a sudden you wanted me. And since we bringing other people up, aren't you expecting a kid?"

"Man, those kids ain't mine."

"KIDS?" I questioned. To my knowledge he only had one woman pregnant.

"Yea both of those bitches just talking." I had to laugh.

"Really Jordan. Everyone out here wants a baby by you?"

"To be honest, yes. They see I'm rich, handsome and we both know I'm great in bed. Why wouldn't they?" He was so full of himself.

"Goodbye Jordan."

"Zia, stop acting like you don't want me."

"Acting? Jordan I'm with someone now and he treats me a hundred times better than you ever have."

"You can't be talking about the thug nigga who has a baby on the way. The one who left you unattended to be attacked."

"No one knew that man would come after me, however; you barely ever visited my job so how would you know if anyone ever came after me?" Complete silence.

"Exactly! So don't question me about anything. Go back to your baby mamas and lose my number." I disconnected the call and plopped down on the chair.

I was aggravated and most of all, pissed for even speaking to him. I never should've answered because all he does is criticize and speak highly of himself. I never paid it any attention but when you're not with that person any longer, you begin to notice everything.

People would think he's obsessed over me but that's far from the truth. Jordan doesn't like to lose and once I left him, he lost out. I may not be those model type women he likes, but I am a damn good woman in my own way and my new man, lets me know every second of the day.

"I don't know why you let him get to you." My mom handed me a glass of iced tea and took a seat next to me.

"I don't either." I drank the tea and sat the glass on the table.

"Are you sure moving in with him is what you want? You know, Steph don't mind you living at the house." I smiled listening to my mom try and get me to stay.

Steph moved my mom into this huge five-bedroom house and brought her a new car. The two of them finally made it public as far as being a couple and it could be because he got her pregnant.

Yes, my 44-year-old mom is having a damn baby. My kid's aunt or uncle will only be a few months younger. Don't get me wrong, I love my mom and will love my sibling but it's weird as fuck to see her pregnant.

Steph didn't have any kids so when she revealed it to him, he damn near cried. My mom almost had a heart attack because she always said, no more babies were coming outta her. I guess when you meet a man you love, all that *Not Me* shit goes right out the window.

Now with me being pregnant, Mazza has been driving me crazy about lifting, sleeping, eating and even working. It's annoying and fun at the same time. Annoying because he won't let me do shit but fun because I can act like a baby and get away with it. He doesn't seem to mind and I love the way he caters to me. It's been a very long time since I had someone loving on me and I'm enjoying every moment.

I still have yet to meet his family though. We were supposed to go over there the day Tionne woke up, but never made it. A lotta shit kicked off with Tariq, Fazza getting arrested due to Ty's mom, and now Mazza is looking for Riley. He said she had something to do with his mentor getting killed but he doesn't know what and wants answers. His cousin was going to tell him, yet; he hasn't been to see her because we've been moving and trying to get into the new place.

I didn't know that Mazza already had a house in Delaware and was waiting on the closing date. Somehow, he was able to get them to push it up and here we are, moving things out this house to go there. I didn't really need anything except clothes and important paperwork. The furniture, and everything else is going to be sold with the house.

It's crazy how I just got comfortable in it and now it's back on the market. I do reap the benefits though because the sale of the house is all my money. And Mazza said, I could go crazy buying new stuff for the house because we aren't ever moving out of it.

"I'm positive ma and before you ask, I'm very happy." She smiled.

"It took a long time for me to get back to this place and I have Mazza to thank for that."

"I think you've thanked him well, don't you think." She patted my stomach that seemed to be getting bigger by the day.

When I was in the hospital, we found out I was almost four months and since then, it's like my belly has grown an inch everyday. Ty is five months and she said Fazza already asked her to take a leave of absence. You know she's not tryna hear it. Matter of fact, I have to stop by and see her. It's been a minute.

****

"What up chicka?" I asked Ty when she opened the door. She looked tired, worn out and stressed.

"I have a lot going on girl. I can't even tell you." She stepped to the side so I could come in.

"Well, Mazza is working all day and since I have no job and nothing to do, I have all day."

"No job?" She closed the door.

"Yea. After being attacked I put in my two weeks and not because of Mazza." She folded her arms.

"I'm serious. That guy put fear in my heart and I refuse to live like that. Then, I have Jordan pretending to love me all of a sudden and I'm scared he'll show up and show out too."

"Good answer."

"Ugh, this is not family feud." I hated watching that show. My mom loved it and would always answer the questions and if they were wrong she'd say, only white people answered them because black people don't talk like that.

"What about a job?"

"Fortunately, my man told me I didn't have to work but there's no way I'm sitting around doing nothing all day."

"Do you know how to do secretarial work?"

"That's answering phones, filing and shit like that, right?"

"Yea, pretty much."

"Yea. I can do that why?"

"There's a secretary job open at the hospital. I'm pretty tight with the lady in personnel. If you really wanna work I can put a good word in."

"Really?" I was low key happy because after high school all I did was fast food places and then Dunkin Donuts.

"Yup. Let me text her and.-"

"Wait!" I put my hand over hers.

"I never went to college and I've only done burgers and donut places."

"Ok. One... I'll help you do a resume. And two... who the hell cares? You're smart Zia, and you were the store manager at a fast food place. You had to do schedules, payroll and all that. Shit, she may put you somewhere else."

"Oh my God. I have to go shopping for new clothes."

"Relax Zia. You'll be wearing scrubs unless you're in one of the business offices, in which I'll ask about that too. And if not, jobs open up all the time in hospitals and employees get first dibs."

"Thanks, so much Ty. I really appreciate it. I can't wait to tell Mazza."

"Girl you ain't hired yet." We both shared a laugh as she sent the text out. I had my fingers crossed because I've always wanted a business-like job. Scrubs or not, I'll take whatever they're offering because I am not sitting on my ass all day.

"Ok, she told me to send over your resume, she'll look at it and call you in for an interview." I told Zia who almost chewed her nails off waiting for Carmen in personnel to respond.

"Shit! I don't know how to do that."

"Girl if you don't relax." I stood up and walked into the second bedroom of my house, that I've turned into an office.

"Damn bitch. This is nice." She surveyed the room. It had a big cherry wood desk in it with an Apple desktop and printer. There was a recliner chair and a 50-inch television in there too. Whenever I needed to bring work home, or do my school work, I never wanted to do it in my bed so I converted this into my office. The third bedroom is going to be the baby's room.

"I don't even wanna discuss the big ass house you're moving in to." She sucked her teeth.

Fazza told me prior to Zia coming here, Mazza had already been looking for properties. He knew Riley was cheating and once he kicked her out, he wouldn't stay in the house. He also said, his brother didn't want another big house but got one anyway because it would be the house his wife and children grew up in. Who knew Zia would be the one; but then again, I had no clue Fazza would be a permanent fixture in my life either.

"It's not that big."

"Oh, seven bedrooms, five bathrooms, a basketball court, and man cave isn't that big. And let's not talk about the.-" She cut me off.

"Ok I get it. I told him it was too big but he said, he's not moving again and I had to get used to it." She shrugged her shoulders.

"Can you believe we're about to have kids by two of the most ignorant and dangerous men around?"

"I don't know what you're talking about. My man is not dangerous."

"Hell, if he ain't." I reached behind the desktop and turned on the switch.

As it powered on, I noticed my mom calling and ignored her again. She's been trying to get in touch with me nonstop and I haven't answered. If I did, all the questions I wanted to know she'd have to answer and most likely she won't. I was trying my hardest to stay away and avoid her stressing me out.

My mom hasn't always been a bitch. She's had her times like all moms but it's never been this serious. I mean, she's accusing Fazza of trying to rape her and regardless; of me not being there, I know for a fact he wouldn't touch her. My mother can be mad all she wants but I definitely have my man's back on it.

The reason I won't answer is because like I said, she'll refuse to answer me, blame Fazza and spit hate the entire time and I don't feel like hearing it.

"Mother problems?"

"You have no idea." I sat down in my computer chair and had her grab the bar stool from the corner. If Fazza came over and I was working, he'd sit on it and watch television until I was done.

"Fill me in. Hold on. Let me order lunch first." She asked what I wanted and placed the order.

The food arrived just as I completed her resume and emailed it to Carmen. She didn't have a lotta job history but I spiced it up for her and sent one to her as well. That way she'll always have it.

"Damn!" Is all she said after revealing everything about my mom and Fazza.

"What you gonna do?"

"I have no idea. Fazza doesn't want me anywhere around her but I need answer. Matter of fact, let's go." I tossed my food.

"Where we going?"

"To my mother's."

"Ughhh." She sat there.

"Just come on." I could see her hesitating.

"I thought you said, Fazza told you not to go."

"And he knows I don't listen. Plus, who's gonna tell?" I stood there staring.

"Bitch, I ain't no snitch." She tossed her food in the trash.

"Ok then. Let me grab my keys."

"Mazza is gonna kill me. This better be worth it." She blew her breath and followed me out to the car.

****

"Why are we sitting in front of a burnt down house?" Zia asked and continued looking around the area.

I sat there in shock because I knew damn well Fazza did this. My mom was super careful when it came to fires. She had one as a little girl and always said, that's her worst fear. Therefore; before we left the house, she'd always check the stoves, make sure almost everything was unplugged and even turned every light off.

I asked her to move after my father died and she refused because we've lived in this house for years. All our memories; pictures, memorabilia and everything else we cherished; gone. Granted, I had some pictures, my yearbooks and other stuff but the majority of my father's things were here.

"This is, well, was my mother's house."

"Oh shit. Why you ain't tell me she had a fire?" We got out and I ripped the caution tape down. I don't know what I expected to see or even salvage, yet; I still went to look.

"Girl, you crazy. I ain't walking over there." I waved her off and stood there crying. How can I not be upset when this is my childhood?

"Tyler, is that you?" One of the neighbors called out to me. I made my way to where she stood.

"What happened?" I asked and she gave me a hug.

"You want me to be honest?"

"I would appreciate it." The woman glanced around the neighborhood and walked me back to the car where Zia was sitting with the door open.

"Your mom has been obsessing over some guy she said, you were with."

"Obsessing? I'm lost."

"Long story short. Whoever this guy is, kicked the doors off your mom's house, cursed her out over you, the cops came, he threatened her and left."

"How long was he here?"

"Maybe five minutes if that because a detective showed up and escorted him out a few minutes later." I knew he didn't touch her.

"Are you sure?" Zia asked.

"Yup because me and my husband were taking a walk." She said it in a way to let us know she was positive about what she saw.

"Anyway, she had me come over the next day and explained what went down and how she's gonna do everything to get you away from him."

"Did she say what?" I asked.

"No and I didn't ask because I wanted no parts in it. If a man is kicking her door in and threatening her, I can only imagine what's next." She pointed to the house.

"Did you see what happened?" I asked regarding the fire.

"The night of the fire, I was bringing my puppy in and two guys were here dressed in black from head to toe. The masks were even black and revealed nothing. They tossed something and I assumed it was a rock, so I closed my door to mind my business."

"Really? Two men dressed in all black and you assumed a rock?" Zia questioned her and had her hands on her hips. She ignored Zia and finished telling me.

"Ty, I look at your mom as a friend but I'm not getting in no mess with her. I'm old and trying to stay on this earth as long as possible. She can fool with these thugs but she won't bring me down." I shook my head. I couldn't even be mad for protecting herself.

"Five minutes later, we heard screaming and looked out the window. The entire house was engulfed in flames and burning quick. Whatever they threw in there had to be flammable because I've never seen a house blow up like that."

"Blow up?"

"Yup. It was halfway burnt and outta nowhere there was a small explosion and BOOM! The house was gone." She placed her hand on my forearm.

"Your mother is mixed up with the wrong person. Ty, she needs you or this person is going to kill her."

"Don't you think he would've done it already?" She smiled and patted my shoulder.

"Even I know he's toying with her."

"Huh?"

"Chile, you better watch these murder shows. He's gonna make her paranoid and let her then think he's finished. When she least expects it, he's gonna kill her." She walked backwards to her house.

"Either hide her or get ready for a funeral. Have a good day ladies." I looked at Zia who had a surprised look on her face. I turned and saw my life flash before my eyes.

"Didn't... I... tell yo ass... not to come here?" I popped Ty on the back of her head multiple times to get my point across.

I keep telling her someone is always watching, yet; here she is in the exact spot I asked her not to come to. Its not like I'm tryna control her, but Ty's mom is a problem and I can't take the chance of her, making Ty lose the baby. I don't understand why my girl doesn't see it the same as I.

"Stop it Fazza." I didn't have to say anything to Zia because Mazza had her hemmed up against the car asking why she even agreed to coming with Ty.

"You so got damn hard headed. Get yo ass to the car."

"How did you know I was here?"

"I got a tracker on you and your car." She sucked her teeth and I pushed her in the direction of the car and stared at the house.

"I did a good job right?" I smiled at me handy work. There was nothing left. I mean, even the foundation was gone.

"Really?"

"Hell yea, really? You know how hard it is to pull a fire off without security catching you? And, I had to pay my tech guy good money since it was late at night and I made him get outta bed."

"But she could've died."

"She didn't tho, yet." I smirked.

"All my memories and..."

"Shut yo crybaby ass up. You have pictures and shit at the house. And the memories of your dad are right here." I used my index finger to continuously poke at the side of her head.

"Are you really gonna kill her?"

"Yup! Now get in the car."

"Can I talk to her first? I just wanna know why." I stood in front of her on the passenger side of the door. Mazza already dipped off with Zia, which means I'm driving Ty's piece of shit vehicle. I hated her driving it but she refused to let me get her a new one.

"You know why." I made her look at me.

"Why?"

66

"She don't want you riding this big ass dick." She pushed me away.

"I'm serious. She'd rather you swallow my kids, then have them." She opened the car door.

"I wonder if she knows your gag reflexes are the shit. Babe, you swallow a lotta cum." I kissed the side of her neck before she sat.

"I'm done Fazza. I'm tryna be serious and you making jokes." I put both of my hands on the side of her.

"One.... those are not jokes; they're facts. And two... who cares why she did it? The fact she was bold enough to not only call the cops, but lie about me tryna rape her, tells me she has to go." She didn't say anything.

"Can you believe she had those people thinking I touched her wrinkled up ass. I mean your mom looks good for her age but I'm sure she has a full gray bush in between her legs. And we both know this dick ain't nothing to fuck with. She'll mess around and break a hip tryna ride me." Ty was mad as hell.

"A'ight. A'ight. Ima be fucking with her for a while so you got time."

"What's that supposed to mean?" She sat in the car and I closed the door.

"It means, I got a few more things I wanna do to scare her and then its lights out." I started the car and pulled off.

I don't care how upset Ty is. Her mom had to go, no if's ands or buts about it. She's not the type of woman you can let slide because she'll do more shit and ain't nobody got time for that.

****

"I don't want a new car Fazza." Ty whined at the Mercedes dealership.

After picking her up the other day at her mother's old house, I drove the Honda and the shit sounded like it was gonna stall out. I got out to look and the bitch was smoking. Ty talking about, it just needs a tune up. A tune up my as. The shit needs to be taking to a dump and shot.

"Fine don't get one but I tell you what." I opened the door to a 2019 Mercedes GLS truck and sat down.

"What?"

"My kid ain't riding in that piece of shit car you got." I was pressing buttons to see how things worked. I must say, this truck was nice.

"My Honda is fine." She stood there with an attitude.

"Yea for a corny person. My baby is going to be high maintenance and a Honda ain't that." I pressed some buttons in the car.

"My babyyyyy." She dragged the word out.

"Will be fine in a Honda."

"First of all, that's my baby and you're just carrying it." I got out the truck.

"And second... the only baby getting in that shitty car is a baby doll."

"You can't tell me what to do." She started pouting.

"Ty, I'm not about to debate this with you." I walked over to the sales guy, who was getting a kick outta us.

"She'll take this fully loaded in plum."

"Oh hell no. I don't want a plum colored truck."

"Thought you didn't want it."

"If I have to drive it, I'm picking the color." She had the guy go over to the truck with her.

"I want Tyler written on the headrest and the driver side mat. I want TV's placed in the back and..."

"You bugging Ty. Ain't nobody say add all that extra shit." I didn't care but I wanted her to realize she acted like a baby the whole time, now she over there demanding shit.

"You want your baby to have the best, right?"

"Yea but shit. I can get the TV's from Best Buy and have them put in. The mats we can get at.-"

"Nope. Money is no object to you so let's get it all done. Oh, and that Mercedes Coup over there." We all turned to look. The shit was bad. It was black with rims and tinted windows.

"Yea, I want that too. K?" She patted my face and continued looking in the truck and then back at me.

"Don't you say a fucking word Fazza and I wish you would say no." She gave me a look and the salesperson looked at me.

"Whatever she wants." I shrugged my shoulders and went to where she was.

70

"Is there anything else your majesty?" I placed my body in front of hers and had her leaning against a different truck. She didn't want anyone putting prints on her new one, as she says.

"Yup. I want a new house, with a pool, playground set and whatever other shit we can get."

"Oh, now you want me to buy all this stuff?"

"It's the only way I'm going to be able to deal with you killing my mother." I heard sadness in her voice and thought about letting her live, but only for a second, and then the thought of killing her was back.

"I know it's gonna be hard Ty and if you want, I won't tell you when I do it, burn her body and be done with it. You can assume she's alive forever and I'll never tell you yes or no."

"You're a dick."

"Shit, I'm tryna help you out."

"Then don't kill her." I busted out laughing.

"Why you laughing?"

"Because your mother wants me to kill her; didn't she tell you?" She had a confused look on her face.

"Fazza!"

"She should've at least mentioned it to you, because the minute she spewed those lies, she made it ok."

"I get it and I wanna know so I can at least give her a burial."

"Fine! But you better not hold out on pussy either." She sucked her teeth.

"And if I do?" She smirked.

"I'll just wait til you go to sleep, lift your nightgown up and ram my shit inside. It'll be too late for you to stop me." I went to leave and she grabbed my arm.

"I may not hold out on pussy but I'm not swallowing." I pushed her back against the truck.

"Oh, you're gonna swallow and like it or I'll spray all over your face."

"Mmmmm, I may like that better." I laughed.

"You my nasty bitch." She wrapped her hands around my neck.

72

"And don't you forget it." We started kissing and heard someone clear their throat.

"Let me go pay for this shit, because we fucking in both of them." She intertwined her hands in mine.

"I love you Fazza."

"I love you too ma and I promise to help you get through it when it's done." She nodded.

I have no doubt in my mind, she'll grieve for her mother and if I could spare her, I would. Unfortunately, her mother went too far and it's no way I can allow her to try and put me in jail, in order to keep me from Ty.

We went in, signed the paperwork and paid. The vehicles were going to be delivered this weekend to the new house she knew nothing about. Hell yea, I'd do anything for her. It's the least I could do after what I put her through. She better appreciate it though, because I'll have her living on one side of the house and me and my baby on the other.

"What ya doing babe?" Zia asked and ran her hands down my bare chest from behind. I was sitting in the living room watching television. This new house was nice as hell and the way she decorated it, made it even nicer.

I wanted to build a brand-new one but this is only three years old. The people who had this built, couldn't afford the mortgage and placed it on the market at just the right time. It had everything we needed and five acres in the back. If Zia ever wanted a brand new one, we definitely had the space to do so. And I'm saying she can because her name is on the deed too.

See, after Tariq attacked her, I refused to allow her to stay anywhere away from me. I had to make sure no one would be able to get to her again because they were looking for me. Granted, the area I purchased her house in was nice, however; her job seemed to the be the place anyone could locate her. Therefore; I had her give a two week notice and brought her here.

She wasn't happy about not working and I told her she never had to but Zia wasn't having it. She said and I quote, *"I am not about to sit around doing nothing all day."* I planned on giving her a position at my job but Ty found her one and she seemed excited about it.

I loved how she was a go-getter and didn't wanna let someone take care of her. She had no choice in the matter because I was doing it regardless, but at least I knew she was about her shit. If only I met her sooner, my ass would've been married with kids already.

"About to fuck you, now that you got my dick hard." I took her hand and made her walk around the loveseat I was on and smiled. Not only was she wearing a short ass negligee thing, but her stomach was beginning to poke out farther.

"Who said I wanted you to touch me?" I stood, removed my basketball shorts and boxers and sat down.

"You better not cum on my new couch." She said and placed her knees on each side of me, grabbed my dick and slid down.

"Mmmmmm. Fuck, it always feels like the first time Mazza." Her head went back as she circled her lower half on me.

"Fuck this couch. We can get a new one." I lifted her up, turned around and laid her on it.

"I love this one tho. Oh my God baby." I watched as her cream oozed out, covering my dick like usual.

"Too bad." The two of us fucked all over the living room and ended up in the bed.

Zia and I may not have started this relationship out the way most couples do, but she is definitely gonna be in my life for a long time. It's sad to say, I thought Riley would be here and had she not strayed, she probably would be. However; it wasn't in either of our future's. She's sleeping with someone else, slept with one of my ex workers and come to find out, she may have something to do with Shakim's death. If she did, I may feel bad afterwards but I'm killing her too.

What's weird is, I did expect to see Riley once she didn't hear from her parents. She was pretty close with her mom and they spoke daily. Unless she snuck in town, no one has seen or heard from her. It didn't matter because I'm taking a ride to Maryland in a few days anyway.

****

"Mazza what's this?" Zia held up a CD, along with the envelope I got from Shawn. We just came in from food shopping. I wanted baked ziti and we didn't have everything for it.

"The envelope is from Tionne's boyfriend but I don't know where the CD came from." I had been meaning to go through it but hadn't had the chance with everything going on.

"It was in the mailbox when I checked the mail. You know I'm waiting for my last check and this envelope has been here for a few days now." I chuckled.

"Why you worried about that little ass check? You don't want for nothing." She placed her hands on her hips.

"What? You don't."

"I still like to have my own money. It's the reason Ty got me a job." I walked over and pulled her close by the string hanging on her sweats.

"That's why I love you even more."

"Mm hmm."

"I'm serious. You left your job, moved with me, about to have my baby and still managed to find a job that's willing to let you start pregnant."

"Mazza, I appreciate all you do but I wanna do things for you too. I wanna pay for dinner sometimes, buy you clothes and sneakers, and pay for groceries and things like that. I want our relationship to be 50/50."

"I get it but don't be mad when I want sneakers that cost $300 or a belt I may want from Ferragamo that will cost $400." She rolled her eyes.

"That's too much money on a belt."

"Oh and $800 ain't a lot on shoes?" I was referring to the red bottoms she saw online. She didn't ask for them but I knew she liked them. I also knew, her ex was using things he purchased against her. If I wanted to do things for her it would have to be at a slow pace.

"They are, which is why I'd never buy them." She pecked my lips and took the CD in the living room.

"Babe, I think this is a DVD." She placed it in the Blu-ray installed on the side of the television and waited for it to load. I sat on the couch and finally opened the envelope Shawn gave me. It wasn't that I took my time, I forgot about it until she reminded me.

I opened it and pulled out a shit load of papers. I felt Zia sit next to me and her hand was on my thigh. Seeing the photos of Shakim's body did something to me and she must've noticed because she took them out my hand. She didn't know a lot about my affiliation with him but she knew enough to know how close we were.

"I want you and your brother taking over when I marry your cousin." Shakim said and handed us a drink. We were at the bar having drinks and shooting pool.

"Why can't you continue doing it?" Fazza questioned and he smiled. Neither one of us wanted his position because it meant more work and more enemies.

"Because Tionne said I hurt her too much and if she's gonna be with me, I have to leave the streets alone and be home more. No more vacations without her, no more bitches,

and no more cheating or she's done." I started laughing because he was in love with my cousin regardless of his infidelity.

"I don't know man." I wasn't tryna deal with bullshit.

"Just think about it and we'll go from the there." We all agreed and finished playing pool. He went to my cousin's house and that was the last time anyone heard from him. When Tionne called crying, I was in disbelief. How can you see someone one day, and they're gone the next? It's crazy but it happens all the time.

"You ok?" I didn't notice a tear leave my eye until Zia wiped it.

"Yea. These pictures take me back to a dark place." She nodded and turned them over.

"What's that?" She pointed to the TV.

"I don't know. It looks like two cars driving." I shrugged my shoulders and picked up another paper that read, *car was bumped from behind.*

"Oh hell no." I said out loud to myself and continued reading. The car was hit from behind a few times, the side was swiped and ran off the cliff.

"Oh my God." I looked at Zia who had her hands covering her mouth.

"What's wrong?"

"Wait! Is this a movie or real life?" She went to get the DVD cover and there was a regular white sheet on top with no words. I turned it over and there was a small sticky paper on the back. You had to peel that hard piece off to open it.

"If I'm going down, so is she!" Is all it read. Zia and I looked at one another and then the TV.

"What did you see?"

"Ummm. Two cars were driving, one bumped the other one, then drove on the side and it went off a cliff. Hold on. Is that your ex?" She pointed and I couldn't believe my eyes. Riley was standing over a cliff and you saw an explosion at the bottom.

"No, no, no. It can't be." I lifted the remote and hit rewind. I watched as the car collided with the other from

81

behind, then on the side, and again the car swerved off the cliff. It was so many angles I guess from different cameras you had to be paying attention to know it all went together. It's exactly the same thing written in the report but why didn't anyone notice?

I hopped up off the seat and moved closer to the TV to make sure my eyes weren't deceiving me. How did Riley know Shakim and why in the hell did she make him go off the cliff? I had to be missing something but what? Then it came to me. Tionne was tryna tell me at the hospital but Ty came in screaming about Fazza and the shit with Tariq happened. She never got the chance to finish.

"Where you going?" Zia put the papers down and came towards me as I grabbed my keys.

"I'm going to see Tionne. If anyone knows anything, she does."

"Are you sure because?-" She stopped and we both turned around when a guy started moaning.

"Is that..." Zia's mouth dropped open.

"Yup. That's her." I had my face turned up watching my ex give the chief of police head in his office, which then switched over to him fucking her on the desk. Now I understood why no one was taken into custody or brought in for questioning. She slept with the chief to keep it quiet.

"I'm just gonna say this and be done." She walked over and turned it off.

"Your ex was a ho." It made me laugh.

"I see now. You coming?"

"Yea because even though I didn't know him, I want to know what happened too." She had me turn around to look at her.

"Are you sure you're ready to hear it?"

"Not really but if I got this DVD, obviously the chief wanted me to know." She agreed and grabbed her things to come with me.

"Who you texting?" I asked when we pulled off. She was going back and forth. I wasn't worried about her cheating and she did tell me Jordan still talking shit. I'm gonna deal with that when I get to Maryland too.

"Ty. I told her to tell Fazza to meet us there."

"For?"

"He loved Shakim too and I think it's best for both of you to hear the truth." She leaned over and pecked my cheek.

"That's why I love you."

"Oh yea." She had a grin on her face.

"You always know what to do and say in a bad situation."

"I'm just tryna be there for my man like he was for me."

"Always baby." I lifted her hand and kissed the top of it. Yea, she is definitely the woman God sent to me.

"Can we stop and grab food first?" I busted out laughing.

"Whatever." She waved me off. I pulled up at Burger King and ordered for both of us. Shit, I was hungry too.

"Shakim, get down here." I yelled up the steps. My daughter was coming down with her baby doll.

"What is your brother doing?" I asked Shakima and she shrugged her shoulders. Yes, both of my children had their fathers name. He wanted his name to carry on. I don't know what he would've named our other kids, had he not died.

"SHAKIM!" I shouted this time and still nothing.

"Relax babe. I'll get him." Shawn said and told me to sit down. Yelling always made my chest hurt, which is why I don't know why Shakim had me doing it often.

"I'll meet you at the table." He kissed my lips and went to get him. I tried to make sure we had dinner as a family as much as possible. I know once my kids get older those days will be scarce, so I'm tryna savor every moment with them.

"Sorry ma. I didn't hear you." Shakim came down with Shawn following behind shaking his head.

"What?"

"Nothing. I'll tell you later." He kissed my cheek and sat down. My daughter said grace and all of us began eating.

Shawn and I interacted with the kids as always. Our conversations were fun and at times, interesting.

Just as I stood to take my plate in the kitchen someone started banging on the door. I'm not talking about knocking hard. I'm talking about banging like they were ready to kick down the door. Shawn and Shakim hopped up and Shakima ran over to me. I tried to make my son come to me but his ass swears he tough. Especially, with my twin cousins showing him unnecessary shit. And now Shawn is marrying into the family so I can only imagine what he's gonna show him or already did.

"Who the fuck is it?" Shawn mouthed the words sorry. He knew I was trying not to use profanity around the kids. Shakim was peeking out the window.

"It's the twins and their sexy girlfriends."

"SHAKIM!!!" I shouted. He turned around with a grin on his face.

"Sit yo behind down." I made Shakima do the same and stood next to Shawn as he opened the door.

"Hey y'all, what's..." I didn't finish when I noticed the look on their faces. Each of them stepped in without so much as a hello.

"Hi Tionne." Ty spoke and gave me a hug. She introduced me to Zia as Mazza's girl and both of them took a seat with the kids.

"Shakim, if you say anything fresh to my girl, I'm gonna beat yo ass." Fazza said and Shakim stood up.

"Cuz, why you keep sweating me when I'm around her? I'm competition, I know but I'ma wait until she has the baby. But after that..." This motherfucker had the nerve to lick his lips.

"Ima let her do what I said in the hospital." Ty's mouth dropped and Fazza went running after him. I don't even bother them when they get into it. Fazza gets a kick outta my son and vice versa.

"Is everything ok?" I asked and Shawn closed the door.

"Ummm Tionne, we're gonna let Shakima show us her room." The way Ty said it had me nervous. I nodded and waited for Mazza to speak. He had a hateful look on his face. Fazza on the other hand was still harassing my son.

"You got exactly five minutes to tell me how you know Riley, how she knew Shakim and if you knew she killed him." I felt the tears falling down my face. I loved my cousins but if he's questioning me, he most likely knows something.

"I don't know if she killed him because like Shawn said, they're still looking into it."

"She did. How did you know her?"

"How do you know for sure?"

"How did you know her?" He ignored me and repeated his question. I went in the living room and flopped down on the couch.

"She's one of the women he cheated on me with." I put my head down.

"Come again." It's like he didn't believe me. I wiped my face and began telling him the story. Shawn came over and sat on the edge of the loveseat.

"I always had an idea Shakim was cheating but never had proof."

"When did you know?" Mazza asked, still upset.

"I found out one day at the mall when I held his phone so he could use the bathroom. A text message came through from some women asking when he was coming home. I had no idea he was living another life. I confronted him that night and he told me everything."

"And what's that?" Fazza asked walking in. Mazza now had a death look on his face.

"He was with a lotta women but this one in particular was young, dumb and did anything he asked."

"Like?" Shawn questioned. I never really discussed this with him either.

"Put drugs in her pussy, did dope runs for him, had threesomes and a whole lotta other shit. He said, she meant nothing to him and even kept her locked up in that house."

"Wait a minute. You knew this whole time who Riley was and never mentioned it to my brother?"

"I didn't know everything until after the funeral because he never told me her name. It wasn't until the lawyer read the will and mentioned Shakim leaving me all his money, houses and other shit. I didn't know she was still living there because I thought he broke it off with her."

"I'm guessing he didn't?" Fazza asked standing close to Mazza.

"Nope. I made her leave the house, gave some of the stuff in there away and sold the rest. I had no idea about Riley and Mazza until after the first year they were together."

"When did you find out?" Fazza was asking me the questions his brother wanted to know but Mazza didn't seem to care.

"Ma, wanted all of us together for Christmas and once she mentioned Riley's name, I couldn't do it."

"That's fucked up Tionne." Shawn said and sat across from me.

"The moment you found out, you should've told him." I agreed with my fiancé because he was right.

"Mazza, I wanted to tell you so many times but my mom and yours, were boasting about how in love you were with her and.-"

"I DON'T GIVE A FUCK TIONNE! YOU WERE MY GOT DAMN COUSIN. IT WAS YOUR RESPONSIBILITY TO INFORM ME. FUCKKKKKKKKK!" He shouted and punched a hole in the glass table. I stood up and he tossed me against the wall by my shirt.

"You let me be with a bitch who was fucking my mentor, and then me." He was so angry, spit was flying out his mouth.

"I get you didn't know at first but when you did, you should've told me. What the fuck is wrong with you? Did you hate me or something? Who would do that to their favorite cousin?"

"Let go bro." Fazza and Shawn were tryna pry his hands off me. His grip got tighter and I felt like he was about to kill me.

"Oh my God Mazza. What are you doing?" He let go immediately. Whatever trance he was in, Zia broke him out of with her voice. All of us were surprised because it's hard to get him to calm down.

"I love you because you're my cousin but don't say shit to me. Don't call and wish me happy birthday, or just to check up on me. You're foul as fuck and I can't be around without wanting to kill you."

"Mazza, your hand is bleeding." Zia ran off and came in the room with a dish towel and wrapped it around his hand.

"I'm ok Zia." He smiled and kissed her cheek.

"Mazza please understand. I didn't want to interrupt your life until I was sure."

"FUCK THAT TIONNE!" He turned around.

"Do you know what's really sad?" He moved closer.

"What's sad is, if you didn't think she killed Shakim you never would've told me."

"I would've Mazza. Please believe me."

"WHEN TIONNE? HUH? IT'S BEEN YEARS AND I STILL HAD NO CLUE. WHEN WERE YOU GONNA MENTION IT?" I put my head down because I had no clue.

"Exactly!" He walked away and I ran in front of him.

"Mazza." He stopped.

"Get the fuck outta my face Tionne before your fiancé arrest me for murder." He said through gritted teeth. The hate radiating off his body could be felt a mile away.

"I'm sorry." I whispered and moved.

"Damn right you are. A sorry piece of shit, who allowed me to be with a woman who killed your kids father."

"Who killed my father? I thought he died in an accident and ma, why are you crying? Cousin Mazza what happened to your hand?" Shakim came strolling down the steps firing off tons of questions.

"Ask your mother. She can answer all your questions."

"I'm sorry about this Tionne. I had no idea things would get this outta control." I looked up at Zia.

"You told him to come over here?" I felt myself becoming angry and it was gonna be directed towards her and it shouldn't have been.

"No. Something was delivered to our house and secrets were revealed. He said, the only one who could answer his questions were you."

"Was he angry when y'all left?" Mazza was talking to Shawn who tried to get him to calm down. Fazza was listening to us and watching his brother.

"A little, which is why I came along." I saw Mazza looking at me.

"You should've kept him home. All this is your fault."

"My fault?" I could see the shocked look on her face.

"Had you let him calm down, we could've discussed this like adults but noooooo. You wanted to be his ride or die bitch."

"Shakim can you excuse is for a minute?" Zia asked and he looked at Fazza who made him go upstairs.

"Let's go Zia. She dead ass wrong and tryna point the finger." Mazza said, yet she didn't move.

"Let's get one thing straight Tionne. We may have just met and I do wish the circumstances were different, however; don't try coming at me because you were holding in critical secrets." She had the nerve to look me up and down.

"Standing here blaming me when it's your fault he spent all those years with Riley. And the whole time, you knew

94

exactly what she was capable of." She was now in my personal space.

"What if she got mad and tried to or succeeded in killing Mazza? What if she tried to kill you or your kids? So many things could've gone wrong and you held that secret the entire time. So before you blame people for your shit, look in the mirror and blame that person first. Stupid ass bitch." She went to turn around and I felt my arm being twisted.

"I may love you Tionne but don't put your hands on her." Shawn said and moved me back.

"What?" Zia turned to look at me.

"What type of woman tries to sneak a pregnant woman?" Ty asked with a disgusted look on her face.

"I'll tell you. A weak one. One who knows she's dead ass wrong and doing anything to make people forget her fuck up but I got news for you love. Mazza won't forget what you did and if you thought in the near future we could be cool; cancel that. I'd never be friends with someone like you." She grabbed Mazza's hand.

95

"Come on baby. You're gonna need stitches." He gave me a stare than ran straight through my soul. I had no doubt he'll return and get in my ass again.

"She was about to whoop yo ass T." Fazza joked on his way out the door.

"By Ty." She rolled her eyes.

"Oh, you're not talking to me?" She turned around.

"I felt bad and tried to understand your position all the way up until you tried to come for Zia. Then, you were about to sneak her. Tionne I can't get down with anyone who'd fight someone pregnant."

"You lucky I was standing in front of Mazza because he was about to light your ass up." Fazza said, shaking his head at the same time

"What the hell were you thinking?"

"It's her fault he came here mad."

"Actually, you need to be happy she came."

"And why is that?"

"Shit, you saw Shawn and I were struggling to get him off you but hearing her voice, snapped him out of it. The way I see it is, if she didn't come, you probably would've lost oxygen from him choking you to death and on your way to the hospital." I looked over at Shawn who had disappointment on his face.

"Zia and I may have just become close but know that I'll have her back right or wrong." Ty said on her way out.

"In this situation you were wrong and need to check yourself. The hate you feel towards yourself for not telling, you're taking out on others and that ain't cool. Come on Fazza, I'm horny."

"Welp! I gotta go." He had a doofy grin on his face.

"What you should be doing is finding Riley for killing him." He was on his way out the door.

"Oh, and if you ever keep a secret like that again, you won't have to worry about my girl or Zia. I'm sure Mazza and I will have no problem taking turns in making you suffer." He put up a peace sign and slammed the door.

I glanced over at Shawn on the couch and felt like shit. Why didn't I tell Mazza about Riley? I knew who she was and let him be with her. What if she killed my cousin like Zia said? I would've never forgiven myself.

"I'm going to bed." He said and rushed past me. I didn't try to stop him. I went in the kitchen to grab a broom and dustpan to clean up the glass Mazza broke.

"You need help?" I looked up and Shakim was standing there.

"It's ok son."

"Why didn't you tell me about the Riley lady?" My son was smart as hell.

"The same reason I didn't tell anyone. I wanted to be sure she killed your dad."

"You still should've told cousin Mazza ma. She was living with him and could've hurt him." He was becoming upset and I understood. My cousins were stable in his life since birth and even though Shawn is around, he still looked to them like fathers.

"You're right and I'm sorry." I finished cleaning up the glass and he helped me take the table to the curb. I locked the door, cleaned the kitchen and went to my room. Shawn was

98

lying in bed watching television. I grabbed my towel to shower and left him right there.

"Do you have any more secrets I should know about?" He asked and stepped in behind me.

"No. I wanted to tell you but I didn't want you mixed up in my drama." He swung me around.

"Your drama, is my drama T. You had the responsibility to tell them so you can't get mad at their reaction. And then you tried to attack Zia. What were you thinking?"

"I wasn't." He grabbed the soap.

"You can forget about going to family BBQ's with them."

"I don't even care anymore Shawn. As long as I have you and the kids, I'm fine."

"You and I both know that's not true. You're going to miss them." I started crying.

"Give them time Tionne." I nodded and stood there as he washed me up, dried me off and carried me to bed. I loved this man with all that I have and if my cousins never speak to me again; I'll be hurt but I'll get through it with him by my

side. I snuggled up next to him and went to sleep.

BOOM! I kicked the front door off the hinges and moved throughout the house in search of this bitch. It was pitch black and the only light came from outside. I opened the bedroom door and there she laid, asleep without a care in the world. I hit her hard with the butt of the gun. Not too hard though, but enough to wake her up. My beef isn't really with her.

"Where the fuck is she?" I placed the barrel of my gun on Evelyn's temple as she laid there in fear.

"Mazza?" I heard and looked on the side of her. One of the guys who worked for me asked.

"Armad, what you doing here?"

"She's my girl."

"Your girl?"

"Yea my girl. We've been together for over a year. What the hell is going on?" He stood up and shut the light on. Thank goodness he had sweats on because I did not wanna see him free balling.

"Your girl knows why I'm here." He came over towards me.

"Look, I know you're my boss but I can't allow you to hold a gun to her head. Put that shit to mine." He stood in front of me making my gun point at his chest.

"Damn, she got you strung like that?"

"Same way, your girl got you. I'm sure you'd be doing the same." Everyone knew about Zia because they've seen us out. They also said my attitude and demeanor is calmer. I guess it would be when my life is peaceful.

"I respect that. Evelyn get up and meet me in the living room." She nodded quickly.

"What the fuck did you do?" I heard him asking in the room.

"I don't know. Baby don't let him kill me. I'm pregnant."

"What?"

"A'ight y'all. Talk about that shit later. I got things to do." I shouted and looked at Fazza in her refrigerator.

"Really nigga?"

102

"What? Evelyn can cook her ass off." I laughed. We never had a problem with Evelyn and have been here a few times picking up Riley and chilling, in general.

"If this goes left, don't kill her. I'll take her punishment." Armad said and sat Evelyn on his lap.

"Tell me what you know about Riley and don't leave nothing out." She took a deep breath and began telling us about her seeing some guy she kept a secret. How Riley did a no call, no show at her job and she fired her. She also said Riley called not too long ago to ask if she could check on her parents because she hadn't heard from them. I asked if she did it and she told me no. She said, Riley demanded it and started talking shit so she hung up on her.

"Did she tell you where this guy lived or what he looked like?" She gave us a description but she could've been speaking about anyone.

"Where is she?"

"Honestly, Mazza. I have no idea and don't care."

"Now you don't care? Y'all are best friends." Fazza said eating ice cream straight out the container.

103

"Really Fazza. That's my favorite." She got up and walked over to him.

"You could've eaten the other kind." She snatched it out his hand.

"What's really good Mazza? Why you put a gun to my girl's head?"

"Your girl used to be best friends with my ex Riley who did some foul shit and I need to find her. The only one who'd have an idea where she could be is her."

"But a gun? You couldn't knock on the door?" He pointed to her shit on the floor.

"Nah and who knew you were with her? You out here being all secretive and shit."

"It's not that. I know she has a professional job and you know what I do. I'm not tryna fuck up nothing for her." He looked at her smiling. This nigga was definitely in love.

"Man, Evelyn don't give a fuck about that. She owns that company. Can't nobody tell her shit."

"I know but.-"

"You do know her and Fazza used to fuck, right?" He turned his head and they were in the kitchen play fighting.

"Oh hell no." He stood up.

"I'm just fucking with you. Fazza is too ignorant for her. It takes a special kinda woman for him and trust me, Evelyn isn't her." I saw him let that breath out.

"Where is she Evelyn?" I asked and she grabbed her phone off the counter.

"This is the last number she called me from." I took the phone out her hand, placed the number in my contacts under DOA and handed it back.

"Let's go Faz." We walked to the door.

"Mazza, I'm sorry she cheated on you and whatever else she did." She hugged me and looked at her door. Evelyn lived in a high-rise penthouse so maintenance was on duty and could fix it in no time.

"Oh Armad." I turned around before walking out.

"I respect you taking up for your woman but don't ever interfere with what I'm doing again." He nodded and Evelyn stood there with her arms folded.

"I don't care about your funky attitude." She sucked her teeth.

"And when my girl sends you a baby shower invitation make sure you show up." Her eyes grew wide.

"Oh my God. You're having a baby?" She ran over and hugged me again.

"A'ight Evelyn. You too close to my boss and I'm not tryna die before my baby born because I'm beefing with him; over you."

"Long as you know." I told both of them goodbye and left.

"So where she at?" My brother asked and closed the door.

"If I'm going off this area code, she's definitely in Maryland somewhere. As long as this isn't a burner phone I'm sure it won't be hard to find her. Even if it is, I'm not stopping my search until her ass is six feet under and that's on my kid." I pulled off I'm deep thought.

I never thought I'd really have to kill Riley but after watching that video again and seeing how she desperately

106

wanted to run Shakim off the road, made me forget the love I used to have for her.

I could care less about her sleeping with the chief, especially after hearing Tariq said he hit it for information. She is the true definition of a woman using what she had, to get what she wanted. And now, I'm gonna be the one to may her regret ever fucking with me.

****

"Did you get the information?" Zia asked when I came in the bedroom. She was sitting up watching television.

"Some. Let me find out you waited up for me." She smiled. It was after one in the morning and she's usually knocked out.

"I wasn't waiting for you per say but I was waiting for something only you can offer." She bit down on her lip and my dick grew.

"I better be the only one who has what you need." She flipped the covers off and revealed her naked body.

"Damn!" I stripped out my clothes fast as hell.

"Always." She slid her bottom half to the edge of the bed, spread her legs and played with her pussy as she gave me some of the best head ever.

"Thanks. I needed that." She wiped her mouth and laid me down on the bed.

"And I need this." She climbed on my face and let me take full advantage of her. She tried to get up after the third one but I held her there. I stared at her after we finished sexing each other down.

"I want you to be my wife Zia." I placed a six-carat, pear shaped diamond ring on her finger.

"Mazza." I shushed her with my finger.

"I know it's been almost a year since we met but I know you're the one. It doesn't have to happen now, but I wanna say, even if you say no, you can't be with anyone else." I rolled on my back.

"Mazza, all I was going to say is I'd love to be your wife."

"You would?"

"It is soon like you said but I know my feelings are real. I don't wanna think about being with anyone else and as far as it not happening soon, cancel that. We can get married tomorrow if you want. That's how serious I am." She rested her chin on my stomach and looked up at me.

"All those years wasted on a woman who wasn't shit, just for God to place the perfect one in front of me." I sat against the headboard and pulled her up.

"You're perfect for me too baby." Her smile lit up the entire room.

"I promise to be the best man I can be for you."

"And I promise to be the best woman for you." We kissed and she laid her head on my shoulder.

"I'm still not fucking with Tionne whether you decide to speak to her again or not. She violated and.-"

"I would never expect you to be ok with what she did because I'm not. I'm sure she'll apologize but I'm not the nigga who expects you to deal with my family because you're with me. I do expect you to treat her the exact way she treats you, and if it's with disrespect, then oh well. All I ask is you don't do it in front of the kids, especially; Shakim. It's bad enough he thinks he a ladies man." She busted out laughing.

"Do you know he said, he could take me and Ty at once?"

"What?

"When we tried to give y'all privacy he was trying his hardest to charm our panties off." She was cracking up telling me the story.

"He is gonna be a piece of work but that's all Fazza. He don't censor his mouth for shit."

"It's cute but I agree about not being disrespectful in front of him."

"The kids are my main concern. And this one right here." I rubbed her belly.

"This one is top priority."

"And what about me?" She fake pouted.

"I'm sorry but you come last."

"So does sex."

"Yea a'ight." I pushed her off and rolled over.

110

"That's ok. I'll just play with myself." I swung my body over so fast.

"That's what I thought. Good night." She turned on her side and rested my hand on her stomach. Yea, I picked the right woman.

"I'm telling you my parents are dead." Jordan looked at me like I was crazy.

"Riley, I think you're overreacting." He stood up and walked to the bathroom. I couldn't help but stare at his backside. Jordan is so damn sexy to me, and now we're gonna have a baby together.

Hell yea, I knew this wasn't Mazza's kid but since we were together, I was planned on making him believe it. Granted, after delivery I'd have to come up with something else but I wasn't worried. Unfortunately, I didn't have to continue with the lie because Jordan accidentally informed me about him and the bitch from Dunkin Donuts I fought.

In all actuality, I believed Fazza was sleeping with her because there's no way my man would stoop so low but then again Jordan was rich too and she was his woman. I can't say she was ugly but she's not Mazza's type that's for sure. He appreciated women who were high class and could fuck him well. She can't be that good in bed if Jordan didn't have any issues cheating on her.

"I speak to my mom everyday and I haven't heard from her." I said following him in the bathroom.

"So, go see what's up. Why you acting nervous?" Could I tell him what I did? He may have cheated on the ex but he did have love for her.

"What's up Riley?" I turned around to see Tariq standing there looking decent. He wasn't Gucci down the way I'm used to seeing him and he needed a haircut.

"What up?" In one swift motion he a death grip on my arm and told me to get in his car.

Now me being the bitch I am, fought relentlessly with him. I punched, kicked and just as I was gonna spit, I felt that steel on my temple.

"I thought you'd calm down. Get yo ass in the car." He made me climb over the driver's seat and sit on the passenger side. Talking about he didn't wanna take the chance of me jumping out when he walked to the other side. I still thought of doing it until he kept the gun on me as he drove.

"Where the fuck is your man?"

"Who knows?" I answered and stared out the window.

He didn't say anything else and pulled up at some barn looking

house. I sat in the car until he yanked me out and pushed me to

the ground.

"You're gonna die anyway so tell me where he is."

"Why you killing me?"

"Because you're the closest thing to him. He don't have

kids and I'll never be able to get close enough to Fazza or his

moms."

"WAIT!!!!!" I screamed and put my hands up.

"He has a new girlfriend and he's in love with her

already."

"Yea right." He cocked the gun back.

"I'm serious look." I showed him a picture of the bitch

I took off Jordan's phone. I planned on taking the ho out

myself but if he's gonna do it, why bother.

"You don't have to believe me but would I really be

showing you another bitch if it weren't true?" I could see him

struggling to see if I were telling the truth so I did what I knew

best. I stood up and began removing my clothes. Say what you

114

want but when someone has a gun pointed at you, morals go out the window.

"What you doing?" He asked with his gun still pointed on me.

"The way I see it is, we both want Mazza to suffer right?" I seductively moved closer and let my hand go in his jeans.

"We may as well hit him hard."

"And how is that?" He put the gun down and let me remove his jeans, and boxers.

"If we fuck, he'll be pissed and if you kill the new chick, he'll be devastated." I dropped to my knees and gave him some of the sloppiest head ever.

"Nah. Don't make me cum." He lifted me by my hair, turned me around and rammed himself inside. Surprisingly, he did a good job.

The two of us fucked the hell outta each other and once we were finished and dressed, discussed how to disable the twins.

Neither of us knew who Fazza's chick was so the best way to get them is through Mazza. Who knew, Tariq would really attack the new chick?

I should be happy he got her but I wasn't because not only is she still alive; the bitch is living in Delaware with him. I only found that out because Jordan spoke to her and she told him. I think it was to hurt him and it did. Jordan can pretend all he wants but like I stated before, he still loved her in some way.

"Earth to Riley." Jordan yelled and smacked me on the ass.

"What? My bad. I zoned out for a minute."

"I see that. Just don't zone out sucking my dick." I sucked my teeth. Is it me or do these niggas love me giving them head.

"Don't act like you don't wanna do it." He stroked himself to get hard and I took over. I'm not sure what's going on in Delaware but I had to sneak there soon to see if my parents are ok.

****

"Why are you here Riley?" Evelyn asked with a snarl on her face. She was leaned back in the chair, in her office judging me. I say that because she's always done it.

"I came to check on my parents. What's up Evelyn? You got something on your mind?" I closed the door and she stood.

"Hell fucking yea I do." She sat on the edge of her desk staring down on me.

"What did you do to Mazza?"

"Nothing why? You know how he gets."

"I do, which is why I almost had a heart attack when he kicked the door down to my house, placed a gun to my head and demanded I tell him where you were." I covered my mouth in shock. If I weren't sure he was searching for me, I knew now.

"I'm sorry Ev. I had no idea." I tried to hug her and she backed away.

"Don't even try it." She walked back around her desk and picked up her cell.

"I told you not to do him dirty because anyone affiliated with you would be affected but nooooooo. Riley does, what Riley wants and doesn't take anything serious."

"How did I know he would do that?"

"It's not about how you knew but more of what did you do to make him?" She tossed her phone down on the desk.

"Have you seen my parents?" I asked trying to deter the conversation.

"You know what's sad Riley?" I started gathering my stuff.

"No but I'm sure you're gonna tell me."

"What's sad is you had a great man at home who allowed you the luxuries of living a more than comfortable life. All he wanted was a woman to love him unconditionally and take care of him. He didn't badger you about working or anything else for that matter; yet, somehow you managed to do the opposite of everything we discussed."

"Well I'm sorry, I can't get perfect like you." She laughed.

"I'm far from perfect Riley but I'm also not stupid, either."

"Stupid?"

"Yea stupid. Whatever you did to that man, has him on a rampage searching for you. I can't even begin to imagine what he's gonna do when he finds you."

"Don't you worry your sweet little head. I'm leaving and never returning." I opened the door.

"I'd pray before walking out the door." She sarcastically said and I turned around to see a smile gracing her face.

"And why is that?"

"Because Mazza should be here in." She looked at the clock on her phone.

"Approximately, two and a half minutes." All of a sudden, fear took over. My body started to shake, hands began to sweat and the paranoia kicked in.

I stared at Evelyn and realized, I lost my best friend because out of all the vile things I've done, she's never turned on me. I'm not saying I didn't deserve her no longer being my friend but damn, she called Mazza, knowing he wants to kill me.

"Well I have a minute to run." I took off out her office, ran down the steps and to my rent a car. The minute I got up the street and stopped at the light, four black SUV's pulled in front of her building.

"Whew! I just made it." I whispered out loud to no one. Sad to say, I never made it to check on my parents and led myself to believe they were dead. They had to be because it's been a few weeks since I heard from them and we've never gone a day without talking; except when Shakim was alive. Mazza could've at least let me say goodbye.

I wiped the tears falling on my way back to Maryland. I had no parents, Jordan didn't know what he wanted to do as far as us being in a public relationship and I'm praying my baby is ok.

All the running I did to get out the office alive, made my stomach ball in knots a few times. I lifted my head to the sky and prayed God hears me begging to keep Mazza away, otherwise; I don't see me or my child making it.

"Can you believe we're having a boy?" Leslie asked and was more excited than me. It's not that I wasn't happy because come to find out the child is mine. Leslie refused to let me deny the baby and had an amniocentesis done early. The doctor suggested she wait due to complications but she did it anyway. Nevertheless; it was confirmed that I'm gonna be a father.

"I guess." I stared down at my phone waiting on Zia to respond. I sent her a text asking if we could meet up and talk. I missed her like crazy. Yea, I treated her like shit but she was the one for me.

"Don't start Jordan." She hopped off the table and began putting her clothes on angrily.

"Leslie, calm your ass down."

"You want me to calm down and you're sitting there without a care in the world about our baby." I looked up.

"What you want me to do, huh? I mentioned on more than one occasion to terminate the pregnancy and you refused so don't come at me because I'm not jumping for joy over a choice you made." I could see her eyes becoming glassy.

"You're sitting her acting like we made this decision together and we didn't. You thought having a child by me would make me want you but it doesn't."

"Jordan."

"Don't Jordan me Leslie. We are gonna co-parent our son and that's it. I don't want you calling me unless it refers to him."

"Are you serious?"

"Dead serious." I opened the door and left her standing there. She drove her own car so she didn't need a ride.

I got in my car mad at the world. I wasn't even mad at Leslie. Zia never text me back and I took my anger out on her. It's unfair but she was the one around me, therefore; she felt the wrath of my attitude. I'm sure she'll contact my mother, ask her to speak to me and blah, blah, blah. Not that anything my mother said would help because she's on my shit list too.

Her and Leslie have become fake best friends and trying to get at Riley any chance they could. I don't know why when my mom met Riley and claimed she was nice and could see them becoming close.

Sometime within the last week, her entire attitude changed towards Riley and she became this bitter grandmother. All she wanted was for me to get her tested early as well to see if the child was mine and have me do drop offs when it's born. At this point, I no longer dwelled on the childish behavior of my mother or Leslie and found myself spending more and more time with Riley.

The two of us met in book 1 as most of you know when I came to Delaware to open my new gym. She claimed to have a man at the time but they were going through complications in their relationship. We exchanged phone numbers and constantly sent text messages, face timed and even engaged in phone sex. I admit, Riley was gorgeous and down for whatever.

When we had our first sexual encounter, I was amazed at some of the things she did to me. Most women wait a while before showing their freaky side but not her. I guess she wanted me to know no other woman could be as good as her.

Little did she know, all women are different in bed. A man can tell a chick she has the best pussy ever and turn right around, fuck another chick and her shit is good and say those exact same words. Hell, women do it all the time too.

Anyway, we continued sleeping together and eventually she popped up pregnant. I asked if it were a possibility for the child to belong to her man, who at the time I had no idea is the one Zia's with. She told me no because they weren't having sex and he strapped up when he did. I chose to believe her because she hadn't lied to me as far as even still living together, so why not?

Long story short, I found out about Zia and Mazza shortly before she was attacked because I went to her mom's one day and he was carrying her out on his shoulder. I followed them and noticed he pulled over. After a few minutes of them sitting there I drove past and what do you know, Zia was riding him in the truck. I was livid and decided to mention it to Riley. She didn't have a reaction and said, it didn't matter because we were sleeping together.

Now both of our exes are in a relationship and living life to the fullest. From what I hear, Zia is expecting and already four or five months, which means she been sleeping with him for a lot longer than I was aware of. I can't say much with two kids on the way but Zia is better than that. At least, I thought she was. I guess you never really know people.

****

"Two babies on the way huh?" My sister said when I pulled up a chair next to her at the bar.

"I know and Leslie is getting on my damn nerves."

"You knew she was a pain from the beginning but what was the reason you kept her around? Let me remind you. *She's only around until I fall in love with Zia.*" She put up air quotes.

"He don't have to worry about falling in love with Zia anymore because that's me all day." I heard and it felt like my nose cracked as the person slammed my face into the bar. I think it's safe to say it's broken. Hearing him say not to worry about Zia, told me this is the guy she's with.

"OH MY GOD! WHO ARE YOU? JORDAN ARE YOU OK?" I lifted my face and blood poured out on my hand. It seemed as if everyone was paying attention.

"I'm his worst fucking nightmare." He spit out and called the bartender over.

"Yo! Let me get four shots of Henney and three shots of Tito's." The guy Mazza said and I turned around to see a guy who resembled him a lot with different color eyes and other men. Who the hell is this nigga?

"Look shorty, if you don't want any parts in this, I recommend you move on."

"I'm not going anywhere. This is my brother." He smirked, looked at the guy with funny eyes and nodded.

"Listen here bitch." He had her by the back of her neck. I could see the tips of his fingers pressing against the side of her throat.

"Brother or not, this ain't what you want. Now move the fuck on." He pushed her away and I saw Karen use both of her hands to catch herself from falling.

"Can I get some napkins?" I asked the bartender who appeared to be shook himself. He tossed some at me and the other one passed out the shots. Each man took one and once Mazza had his, he slammed the glass down and drug me out the club by my shirt. I don't mean across the floor but he definitely had me at a disadvantage. Outside he threw me against the wall and backed up.

"Where is she?" I held my head up to keep some of the blood from leaking.

"Who are you looking for?" I asked.

"You wanna play games." I literally almost passed out from the hit to my ribs.

"I don't know who you want." He went to hit me again and I put my hand out.

"Just tell him what he wants to know Jordan." I heard my sister crying in the distance.

"I don't know where she is."

"Wrong answer." Instead of hitting me again, my sister yelled out. I looked to see the guy with a gun to her head.

"Ok. Ok. She went to Delaware to find out if her parents were dead."

"She didn't stay, which means she returned. This is my last time asking. Where is she?" This time I saw him reaching in his waist.

"If she returned I don't know because I was at the doctors with my other baby mother and then my parents. I haven't seen or heard from her."

"Other baby mother? How many you got?"

"Two."

"Oh yea." Mazza asked with a confused look on his face and standing there in a stance with his arms folded.

"You didn't know Riley's having my kid?"

"I fucking knew that bitch wasn't pregnant by you bro. I felt it every time I took a shit." *Did he just say what I think he said?*

"She told me it was mine."

"I don't know if you care or not but that's my baby. We never used protection and it's the reason I moved her out here."

"Well this is news to me. I thought she left on her own." I thought about laughing and quickly changed my mind. I don't need him hitting me again.

"I wanted her close to raise my baby." He walked up on me, pushed my face up and my head against the wall.

"That baby's not gonna make it." His mouth was close to my ear.

"Tell that bitch I'm gonna kill her slow, then bury her next to her parents." He moved away and stared at me.

"Oh. If you ever dial my fiancé's number again, I'll break every fucking bone in your body. Capeesh!! He threw up the peace sign and all of them packed into black SUV's. All except the one who still had my sister by her hair. I didn't even pretend to not know who he's speaking of.

"Get your brother in line, or you'll be burying him too." He pushed her so hard, her face hit the pavement. Thirty seconds later, all four trucks pulled off. I went over to help my sister.

"GET OFF ME!" She screamed and rolled on her back.

"I'm sorry Karen. I had no idea Riley's ex would come looking for us."

"What did she do?"

"Honestly sis. I don't know but I'm gonna find out."

"What about the baby?"

"I don't know." She stood up, wiped her clothes off and told me to get in her car so she could drive me to the hospital. Riley got some shit with her and when I find her, she's gonna tell me everything.

"I'm buying this for Fazza." I held up the package.

"What's that?" Zia questioned with her face turned up.

"It's called V.I.Poo like a V.I.P."

"Ok but you're still not telling me what it is."

"Duhhhhh!" I pointed to the lady's face on the can. She had a disgusted look and her two fingers squeezing her nose. I looked around to see if anyone was listening.

"This is that spray you use when you're about shit."

"Ok. Everyone uses spray."

"Zia, you spray this before you go and it's supposed to make it so no one knows you're even going. We all know my man can pollute the air like crazy when he uses the bathroom." Now she really had a gross look on his face. She took the package out my hand and read the back.

"That's good and all but what you gonna do about; what did he say, "*his big ass dookey that don't break and clogs the toilet?*"

"Ugh ah ho. Don't come for my man."

"If you saw what I saw in the bathroom at my old job, you'd understand." She waved me off and pushed her cart ahead of mine. We were both grocery shopping for our own houses. Her mom and Steph were visiting for the week and she couldn't wait to cook a big dinner in that humongous kitchen of hers. Even though Mazza wasn't sure Zia would agree to moving in with him, he still picked out a nice spot.

"Are we ever gonna have the dinner at Ms. Chambers place?" Zia asked putting Adobo seasoning in her cart. With everything going on, she still hadn't met the twins mom in person. They've spoken over the phone a lot but anytime they were supposed to meet, things always came up.

"I talked to her yesterday and she wants to have a small BBQ."

"That sounds nice."

"It's what I thought until she mentioned Tionne attending." Zia stopped and turned around.

"You can count me the fuck out." I busted out laughing.

"Why can't you come with me and we'll both sit there talking shit about her."

"Petty much?" She smirked.

"All day, every day."

"I don't know Ty. I already discussed with Mazza I can't fuck with a bitch who doesn't take responsibility for her own shit."

"I get it Zia but don't send me alone. You know if I even thought about tryna miss it, Fazza will drag me kicking and screaming. I swear, he's a got damn mama's boy."

"Is that why he used to love sucking on my tities? I'm telling you that man definitely knows his way around my body." I knew the voice and hated that I was pregnant at the moment.

"Don't say a word Ty. She's tryna get a rise outta you." I never turned around and continued in the next aisle, only to have this bitch following.

"You do know I'm gonna get Fazza back, right?" I turned around and laughed in her face. That is until she rubbed her stomach that appeared to be almost the size of mine.

"Oh yea. How is that?"

"It seems like those pills were defective he had me take and that was about five and half months ago I think. Looks like we'll be sharing a baby daddy boo."

"Yea right. I'm a nurse who you fooling?"

"I'm not fooling no one sugar. Next time you go to work, or even online; look up defective plan b pills and the company. The ones he forced me to take is from that company and they're being sued by tons of people because of the pill not working. Me, however; I'm sending them a thank you card." She had a big cheese on her face and Zia stood there in shock with me.

"Not a problem Shanta. But let's make something very clear."

"Don't say it Ty. She's recording you." Zia pointed to her phone and sure enough she had it facing outwards and even though the camera was facing the floor, you could see the numbers moving at the top proving she was indeed taping us.

"Get your nosy ass outta here." She said to Zia who snatched the phone out her hand and stopped it.

"Bitch we all pregnant. I'll beat your face in and let Ty stomp this baby outta you. Keep playing." Zia threw the phone and hit her in the face with it.

"Ma'am you have to leave." The manager came over and said to Shanta.

"Why am I leaving? She..."

"I saw you watching these women before coming over here. If they're this upset it's because you did it. I'm sorry but I can't have you in here harassing my customers. Don't make me call the cops."

"Fine! Tell our baby daddy I'm gonna need a bigger place and some stuff for the baby's room." She stuck up her middle finger and waddled out the door.

"Let's finish in here and deal with everything else later." I just broke down crying. Zia grabbed my hand and asked the manager where the bathroom was.

"Ty, don't let her see you like this. Get it together." She handed me paper towels.

"I swear if that's his baby, we're over."

"Ty you took him back after he cheated."

"Yes, but there was no baby involved; not even a possibility. It's not the same Zia."

"Ok. Ok let's just go." I nodded and both of us walked out the store with no food and went our separate ways. If it's true, I'm leaving him for good. I don't care what anyone thinks. I'm not helping him raise no kids but our own.

****

"Hey baby. Let me tell you what happened in Maryland." Fazza strolled in the house and removed his clothes as he went into the bathroom to shower. Him, Mazza, crazy ass Kelly and a few others went down in hopes to find Riley. They were going to kill Jordan but since he showed no signs of plotting on Mazza, they changed their minds.

"TY!" He shouted and I continued ignoring him. I heard the shower cut on and not even ten seconds later he was pulling me out the bed.

"What the fuck is wrong with you?" He led me in the bathroom, stripped me right outta my pajamas and made me get in. I could've fought him but for what? Him to manhandle me? I wasn't in the mood.

I stood there with my arms folded on top of my belly watching him lather the soap on his body. He did it a couple of times, washed his face, rinsed the soap off and shut the water off. I looked at him as he stepped out, grabbed the towel and wrapped him up.

"Oh you're not gonna wash me up?"

"Nope. Do it yourself."

"FAZZA!"

"Oh now you wanna talk? When I brought you in the shower you should've opened your mouth." I sucked my teeth, grabbed the soap and washed up. I didn't need to because I had taken a shower, two hours before he got home but now that I'm in here, I may as well.

I stepped out, walked in the room and he wasn't on the bed. After throwing my clothes on, I went to see where he was. Do you know he was laid out in one of my guest bedrooms, watching television and eating his food I left in the microwave? I stood in front of him and he moved me over to look at the TV.

"Aren't you gonna ask what's wrong with me?"

"Nope. If you wanted me to know, you would've called or acted like a woman and approached me the right way." He looked at me.

"You know I'm not about no fucking guessing games and I wish you would cry." I tried to wipe the tear threatening to fall. Anytime he got stern with me, I would bust out crying. This baby, had me being one.

I plopped down on the bed and laid my head on his shoulder.

"If she has your baby, we can't be together." He muted the TV and made me sit up.

"What the hell you talking about?"

"Shanta."

"I thought we discussed this shit already. Ain't no one having my kid but you."

"Fazza, she came in the store with a big belly talking about the pills you made her take didn't work. She said, if I don't believe her to look online because there's a big lawsuit going on about it."

"This was today?" I nodded my head.

138

"Move." He stood and walked out the room.

"Where you going?"

"To finish this bitch." I followed him in the master bedroom to see what he was doing,

"She's pregnant."

"You think I care?" He pulled his t-shirt over his head.

"I'm not about to come home to fuck my girl and can't because this bitch found a way to piss you off."

"Are you serious?"

"Hell yea I'm serious. Do you know how many bitches tried to fuck and I swerved them because my woman has the best pussy out there?" I ain't gonna lie. A bitch had a grin on her face.

"Then I come home to tell you how it went, only to be ignored and told you're gonna leave me over some bullshit." He stopped and looked at me.

"And put this fucking ring on because we're getting married one day." He pulled out this huge light blue diamond and slid it on my finger. I mean it was beautiful.

"Fazza."

"I don't wanna hear shit Ty. Just have your got damn jaws ready when I get home because you're gonna be sucking for a long ass time." He stepped out the room and I was still in awe of the diamond.

I finally pulled myself out the daze and tried to make it downstairs but he had already left. What kind of proposal is that? At this point, I don't even care. I'll take it if it meant us being together, forever.

I laid in bed massaging my jaws. He knew how to keep himself from cumming, so I know it's gonna be a long night and I'll have a sore face in the morning but he's worth it.

Fazza

I'm over this bitch and her lies. Shanta can accuse me

of being her baby daddy all she wants but we both know it's

not true. The day my girl beat her ass, she went to the hospital

to get checked. Little does she know, I had the nurse do a

blood pregnancy test on her. I wanted to be sure the pills

worked in case Shanta concocted up a lie and I'm glad, I did.

I wanna say, I can't believe she tried to pin whatever

baby it is, on me but it's expected. She's the type who liked

testing me. I usually ignored her like I been doing. However, I

should've taken care of her a long time ago but my focus was

on Ty's mother for the moment. I was doing all types of dumb

shit to her too.

One day, she came out the hotel she was staying in and

Kelly and I, threw a shitload of firecrackers at her. I almost

peed on myself when she fell and started screaming she was

shot. Another time, she was leaving church with her fake

Christian ass and I followed her. She pulled into the store and

got out. I went in, down the same aisle and bumped into her. I

swear, she pissed herself and started screaming for help. I

walked out and waited. This bitch called the cops too. I'm gonna fuck with her a little longer before I take her life.

I parked at Shanta's house, finished smoking and walked to her door. I half expected her to open it but she's probably not expecting me this late. I glanced around and no one was out, which made this even easier. This bitch is bound to scream and since no one's out here, they won't hear. I used the key she kept under the rug for me to get in. She stupid as hell to still have it there.

I made my way up the stairs, and opened the bedroom door. She was turned over on her side running her mouth about the exact shit she said to my girl in the store. I stood there waiting for her to finish and found myself getting angrier. Had I not gotten that test done, I may have believed the story too.

"Hold on girl. This baby on my bladder." She put the phone face down, stood and turned to see me standing there. Her belly was out there.

"SHIT! You scared me." Before opening my mouth, I picked her phone up and disconnected the call. It was only her sister anyway.

"What you tell my girl?" She waved me off and tried to move past me.

"Fuck that bitch. She thinks she's better than me because you got her pregnant. Well guess what? We both having your baby." She said with finality. I snatched her by the hair, wrapped it around my hand, banged her head against the wall about three times and made her look at me. She was dizzy and barely standing.

"I told you to leave my woman alone but you didn't listen."

"I'm sorry." Fear was all over her face.

"Too late bitch." I grabbed the string out my pocket, wrapped it around her neck and strangled her, until her soul descended from her body. I let her corpse fall to the ground, poured the small can of lighter fluid I had in my back pocket on her and used my lighter to start the fire. I always told the bitch, I'd burn her alive but she didn't listen and now look. Her and the baby suffered. *Selfish bitch!* I looked up to the sky and spoke to God.

143

"Lord forgive me for my sins but the way I see it is, you owe me this for not having my back when I slipped up. We even God. Oh yea, thanks for keeping Ty in my life though. I'll say my prayers every night from here on out. Oh wait! I have one more life to take and then I'm done." I called my peoples up to clean this mess up, got in my car and drove home.

"TY!!!" I shouted, slammed the door and locked it. She came rushing out the room in a robe.

"You got those jaws ready?" She rolled her eyes.

"Roll 'em all you want. You better suck my soul out." I walked up the steps and into the room. She had soft music playing and was lying in bed naked. Her legs were spread open and her juices were seeping out.

"As sexy as you look, I'ma still need my dick sucked."

"As long as you handled that, your fiancé is gonna give you whatever you want. Come here baby." She gestured me with her finger and like the strung-out nigga I am, I went straight to her.

"You smell like smoke." She turned her face up.

144

"Oh shit. Hold on." I jumped in the shower and I'm happy to say, my girl joined me and gave me exactly what I wanted and more. Yup, I picked the right person to give my baby and last name too.

∗∗∗∗∗∗∗∗∗∗∗∗

"What type of proposal is that?" My mom asked as she prepared dinner for me and Ty. She wanted company and promised to cook.

"She lucky I even asked, after giving me attitude." I grabbed a pickle out the jar.

"You better be lucky I said yes; well, let you slide it on my finger." Ty waddled her pregnant ass in the kitchen.

"You nosy."

"I'm not nosy. I just know you like to extend your versions of the story. Therefore; I come to make corrections when need be." My mom thought it was funny.

"Whatever. You could've said no or moved your hand but being the brat, you are, you didn't. Plus, you know this dick too good for you to let go."

"Why does everything have to go back to that?" She pointed to it.

"It's the reason you put up with my shit and we both know it." I walked out the kitchen.

"You're so full of yourself."

"And you're full of my cum." I pointed to her stomach.

"In your belly and mouth."

"Ughhhh. I can't with you."

"Yes you can because you love this nigga." I grabbed her hand and stood behind her.

"You love me Ty?" I loved hearing her say yes.

"Sometimes."

"Sometimes huh. How about when I do this?" I sucked on her neck and slid my hand under her shirt to caress her swollen breasts.

"Fazza, your mom is in the other room. Ssssss."

"Come here." I led her upstairs in one of the bedrooms and locked the door.

"I am not having sex in your mom's house."

"Too bad you don't have a choice." I let my pants fall to the floor, along with my boxers. I pulled her leggings and panties down.

"You have the prettiest pussy I've ever seen and it's been a lot." She popped me on the head.

"You got a hand problem."

"No I don'tttttttttt. Oh fuckkkkkk." I had her legs open on the bed as I sucked gently on her enlarged clit.

"I'm cumming baby." Her cream rushed out and into my mouth. I gave her a few more and pushed my way in.

"I love you so much Fazza." I stared down at my fiancé she'd a tear from the euphoric feeling I was giving her.

"I love you too Ty and no one will ever come between us again. Mmph. This pussy is the fucking best." We began kissing and going at it like rabbits. By the time we finished an hour had passed. Luckily, we had clothes here from when we stayed over after the shit with her mom.

"I can't wait until my son comes." She smiled and all I could do is return the gesture. We don't even know the sex of the baby but like all men, I'm gonna say my son.

This woman really had my heart and there was nothing

I could do to get it back. Now I knew what it felt like to be

dangerous in love with someone.

"I'm happy for you Ty." I told her and handed the waitress back the menu. We were in some Mexican restaurant at the mall. She wanted to try it because the only thing she's eaten close enough to this type of food was Taco Bell.

"Thanks girl and I'm happy for you too." I lifted my hand and flashed it over and over.

"You know what's crazy?" I asked and watched as the waiter placed our drinks in front of us.

"What?" She hit the table a few times with her straw to get the paper off.

"This time last year, I was going through so much with my ex, and now here I am about to marry a man who has blessed me with a baby, house and anything else my heart desires." She smiled.

"And lucky for me, the sex is beyond explosive." I smiled thinking about all the ways Mazza handles me in the bedroom.

"Not that you wanna hear about it but Fazza makes my body do things, I didn't even know it could do." I turned my face up.

"He may shit any and everywhere but my man is very clean."

"I'm sure he is but I don't think I'm ever gonna get that sight out my head." She busted out laughing.

"When he buys my new house, I'll make sure he has those fast flushing toilets like restaurants have, so I don't ever have to walk into it."

"What happens if he clogs it? Ty, you CAN NOT prepare yourself for it." She warned.

"He'll be taking care of that." The two of us sat there talking and joking about everything.

I've never been this close to a chick so hanging with Ty is refreshing. Plus, I know she won't ever sleep with my man and vice versa. Even if I didn't meet Mazza first, I know for a fact his brother would've never been anyone I saw myself with. Ty is definitely a special type of woman to deal with a man like him.

I can say he loves the shit outta Ty too and when she left him for cheating, Mazza said he was distraught. I say good for his ass. I'm positive it's a lesson he'll never wanna be taught again.

****

"Zia, you can go once Fazza gets here." Ty said as we pulled up to the doctors. We went out to eat first and I planned on dropping her off but I wanted to see if my predictions were correct.

"Nope! I'm telling you, it's more than one baby in there." She waved me off as we got out the car.

Ty was six and a half months now and I was a month behind her. However, I've seen women pregnant at six months and of course we don't all carry the same but Ty is fucking huge. I keep saying she's having twins but she disagrees and says the doctor would've told her. I keep saying they make mistakes but she's adamant it's only one child. For her sake, I hope I'm wrong. I can't imagine one mini Fazza and to have two at once, would be a mess.

We went inside to sign in and took a seat in the waiting area. There were a few other women and one in particular asked if she were carrying twins at the same time Fazza walked in. He assumed Ty went in the back already and almost had a fit.

He's still mad that when she first found out, she didn't send him no ultrasound photos or invite him to the initial appointment. He told her, she better not try that shit again.

"What up Z?" I waved and put my head down. I can only deal with him sometimes.

"Let me guess. You didn't get no dick before you left this morning." He said loud enough for everyone to hear. This is exactly why I keep him at arm's length.

"Leave her alone baby. You know how grouchy she gets when no Chamber dick is inside her." I slammed the magazine on my lap and looked at Ty.

"Really! You too."

"I have to be on my man's side Zia. If not, he won't grace me with that tongue." He smirked and sat her on his lap, before the two of them went at it kissing like no one else was here.

"Oh my God, you two." They stopped and laughed at me.

"Ima have to get Mazza to dick you down real good tonight. At least it will hold you over for my mom's BBQ tomorrow." I sucked my teeth because I dreaded going there.

"For your information, he doesn't dick me down. I fucks the shit outta him. Hence; why I have a ring." I flashed it in front of him.

"Oh yea." I heard Mazza's voice and Fazza turned his phone toward me. He had my fiancé on FaceTime.

"You play too damn much. Hey baby." I smiled in the screen.

"We'll see who fucks who later." I snatched the phone from Fazza and turned the volume down.

"Baby, I'm still sore from last night." I heard the two of them cracking up.

"Too bad. See ya soon." He smiled and hung up. I tossed the phone at Fazza.

"Tyler Evans." The nurse shouted and the three of us went to the back.

As Ty undressed, Fazza seemed to be preoccupied with his phone, while I was texting Mazza about dinner. He wanted me to cook his favorite because he'll need energy for afterwards. I swear, him and his brother get on my nerves.

"Let's see what we have going on today." The doctor said coming in. I placed my phone down and waited for her to perform the ultrasound.

"Are you experiencing any discomfort?"

"A little on my right side." Ty pointed and Fazza stood behind the doctor as she turned the machine on and squirted gel on her stomach.

"What's that?" Fazza asked pointing to the screen. He's been to the appointments and saw the pictures, but I think this is the first time he's ever asked a question because the doctor and Ty were both shocked.

"Well, what do we have here?" Ty sat up to try and look.

"What's wrong? Is my baby ok?" Fazza had this huge grin on his face before the doctor answered.

"I knew my sperm was the shit. Ty, you got two babies in you. Look!" He was excited as hell. I went over to look and the doctor gave Ty an, *I'm sorry* type of look and shrugged her shoulders.

"You're kidding me, right? Ain't no way in hell I'm having twins."

"Ms. Evans, I deeply apologize for this mishap. The other baby must've been hiding the entire time."

"How could that happen?"

"Believe it or not, it happens a lot. Baby B, will be so far under Baby A, we won't be able to detect it."

"You didn't hear two heartbeats on the machine?" Ty's nurse instincts started kicking in because she was bombarding the doctor with questions.

"Again, if the baby is hidden only one heartbeat will be heard. Do you wanna know what you're having?" Ty had tears running down her face. She knew just like I did, that it was about to be problems tryna raise two kids at once.

155

"HELL YEA! I need to know if I'm having sons and if their dick is gonna drive the bitches crazy." Me and the doctor sat there in shock.

"What? My dick is big and I know they're gonna be blessed with the same." Ty just put her head down.

"Ummm ok. Do you want to know?" The doctor asked Ty.

"I said yes. Now get to it." The doctor wasted no time and did like he asked.

"Ok. Baby A is definitely a boy." Fazza was like a kid in the candy store shouting out *Yes, and I knew it.*

"And baby B is a girl."

"Oh hell no. You need to figure out a way to make that one a boy too."

"FAZZA!" Ty screamed and he snatched the machine around to look again.

"What? Ain't nobody got time for no spoiled ass girl. I need boys to carry on my legacy. Doc, how do we change it?" At first, I thought he was playing but this nigga was dead ass serious.

All three of us laughed so hard, he got mad and told Ty she walking home. He said, if I give her a ride, he's gonna flatten my tires at the house. He slammed the door on his way out. I haven't laughed that hard in a very long time.

"Is he gonna be ok?" The doctor asked as Ty stood to get dressed.

"He'll be fine."

"Are you sure?" She was more concerned than Ty.

"Yes. He always said, he doesn't want a girl because he'll be killing boys everyday for trying to be with her." The doctor thought it was hilarious, where we both knew he meant it.

"Have fun calming him down." She handed Ty a card with her next appointment on it and left.

"Don't you say it Z."

"I told you." She got mad.

"Ok, I won't say it again but you know his mom is going to say the same thing."

"Whatever." We walked outside and Fazza was standing there smoking a blunt.

"Let's go."

"I thought you said, I had to walk." She walked over to him.

"I thought about it and realized it would take you too long to get home. I need to relieve this stress you just caused ASAP."

"I caused?" Ty pointed to herself.

"Yup. It's your fault we're having a girl."

"How is that?" She had her arms folded.

"Because I only shoot boys. You must've done something to change it."

"Bye y'all." I couldn't take anymore. My stomach was hurting from laughing at his shenanigans.

"You're leaving me Zia?"

"You're in good hands girl." She went to sit in the car.

"Ok but when he figures out a way to make my daughter a boy, don't get mad when you can't buy girlie stuff." We both busted out laughing.

"Oh, I'm a joke Ty? Wait, til I get you home." I left the two of them going back and forth in the parking lot. I may not like some of his ways but they are perfect together.

I drove straight home to prepare dinner for my fiancé. I smiled at the thought of even saying it because I never thought a man could treat a woman so well. After dealing with someone such as Jordan, I swore men off but I'm glad Mazza pursued me.

I parked, went in and started cooking. When I finished, I showered and put some night clothes on.

"Now, what were you saying earlier?" Mazza asked when I met him in the kitchen.

"Nothing." He put his fork down and moved towards me.

"Oh you said a lot."

"I'm tired baby."

"Me too but you need to be taught a lesson." He picked the fork up, ate a little more, grabbed my hand to go upstairs and took me to ecstasy more times than I can count.

"I don't wanna go." Zia whined in the shower as I washed her up.

Her stomach was getting bigger and she complained about having to bend down to wash her legs and feet. I had no problem assisting her. I've always wanted kids and even though the baby isn't here yet, I enjoyed having the full experience with her and catering to the crazy demands. She assumed it's only because she's pregnant but I'll do it for her regardless.

"You should've never told my mom yes."

"She made me an offer I couldn't refuse." I lifted her leg slightly to wash her feet.

"You're telling me; her promising to make you greens and baked Mac and cheese did it?" She licked her lips.

"Yup and I can't wait to eat. I've been craving that for a few weeks." She rubbed her stomach as she spoke on it.

"Why didn't you make it?"

"It takes too long and standing makes my back hurt." I shook my head laughing.

The two of them finally met face to face the other day because my mom said she had enough of waiting. She claimed to feel some kinda way that Zia was pregnant with her grandchild and they've only spoken on the phone.

I've met her mom, had dinner and hung out with her plenty of times and it's been almost a year and they haven't ever graced each other's presence.

My mom is very nice and didn't take shit from anyone. She's a realist when it comes to situations and she's gonna give it to you raw, whether you wanna hear it or not. I tell her she reminds me of Zia's mom a lot. They both go hard for their kids and neither of them can wait to meet the baby. And no, Zia's not having twins.

I wouldn't mind and I'm sure we will down the line but we need to enjoy raising one, before two. My brother and Ty have their hands full and I can't wait to meet my niece and nephew. The good thing about it is, my mom is going to stay with them for a few days to help Ty, and Zia's mom is going to do the same here.

"You're being a brat to my mom too huh?"

"Whatever." She took my hand to step out the shower. I dried her off and wrapped the towel around her. We went in the room to get dressed and head out.

I knew Zia wasn't interested in going due to Tionne attending and I felt the same. It's the exact reason I told her not to feel obligated to converse with my cousin just because we're together. People, or should I say family members tend to think, the person you're with has to speak or even befriend them if they're involved and that's far from the truth.

In my opinion, it's actually better for them to stay as acquaintances. That way when we argue, the family won't get involved for the most part or even take sides. I've heard about family becoming cool with spouses and the minute something goes wrong in the relationship, the spouse becomes the most hated person in the world. It's crazy.

"It's a lot of people here." She observed the many cars and trucks on the street.

"I know." My mom was supposed to have an intimate BBQ, yet somehow, it looks like the entire hood is here.

"There's not going to be any greens or mac and cheese left for me." She had her head leaning on the door and I heard sniffling.

"Yo, I know damn well you're not crying." I turned her head and sure enough she had some tears.

"Wait, til I tell my brother." She wiped her face fast.

"Don't you dare."

"Nah, this shit funny. Who cries over food?"

"Mazza, you know I cry for everything."

"But food though?"

"What if it's all gone? She specifically made it for me and it's so many people." I secretly recorded her because no one was gonna believe this.

"Stop laughing Mazza." I couldn't help it.

"Ok. Ok. Let's go in and make sure my two babies have food." She nodded her head and leaned over to kiss me.

"Did you record me?"

"Yup."

"MAZZA CHAMBERS! ARE YOU SERIOUS RIGHT NOW!" I jumped out the car and watched her open the door.

"You better delete it or I'll take this ring off and..." She never finished her sentence because I had her hemmed against the car.

"Take it off and watch what happens." She tried to push me off but my strength overpowered hers.

"You can't make me marry you."

"Hell if I can't. Now get your spoiled ass in the house before I have you walking worse than you already are." And like the brat she was, it's exactly what she did.

"What's the matter honey?" My mom asked the minute she stepped in the house.

"Mazza is making fun of me because I'm gaining weight. He called me fat and.-" My mom cut her off and stared at me.

"Ma, you know damn well I would never say anything like that." She came over to me.

164

"I'm gonna kick your ass if you make her lose my grand baby because you're stressing her out."

"Ma, Zia is..."

"Is what? Huh? You better not say she's overreacting." Zia was standing behind my mom sticking her tongue out.

"And why are you calling her fat? That's your baby doing her body that way."

"I'm not gonna say anything else." I put my hands up.

"You better not. Let's go Zia. I have your food put away so no one can touch it." My mom took her hand and Zia turned around and flipped me the finger. I can't wait to get her petty ass home tonight.

****

"Yoooooo, is she really crying over food?" Fazza and Kelly were hysterical laughing at Zia. She wanted to play games with my mom so hell yea, I'm showing her being a cry baby.

"Then she tells ma, I called her fat and was shaming her."

"Damn, I know ma dug in your ass." Fazza handed me the blunt as we smoked down the street.

My mother would kill us if we smoked around women and kids; especially Ty, and Zia who are expecting. You would think they were her birth daughters by how much she protected them and took their side. I think Ty loved it being her mother was doing the most and won't be around much longer. I guess she getting used to another mom in her life.

"Yea but I'm definitely gonna dig in Zia's ass later; and I mean that literally." Kelly almost choked and Fazza gave me a pound.

"Hell yea bro. Make her regret that shit."

"You already know."

The three of us sat out there for a while smoking and bullshitting. By the time we walked in the house, the music was playing and people were dancing and carrying on. I moved behind Zia and bit down on her neck.

"It's on later."

"I'm staying here tonight."

"You mean we and I'll fuck you in one of the rooms. It don't matter to me."

"You make me sick."

"And I see that ring still on your finger tho."

"It's because I can't get it off." She pretended to wanna remove it.

"Yea a'ight." She turned around and kissed me.

"Maybe, I'll give you some head in the bathroom, if you eat my pussy on top of the car."

"NOW!" She smiled.

"You don't have to tell me twice." I took her hand in mine and walked towards the bathroom.

"I'll handle you when everyone leaves." I opened the door.

"Hell yea you are. I don't give out free head." She smirked and started to unbuckle my jeans before I even closed the door.

"I love going down on you baby." She kissed me and used her two hands to maneuver my jeans down my legs.

KNOCK! KNOCK! Neither of us broke our kiss.

"He missed me." She stroked my man and slid her finger over the tip and placed it in her mouth.

"He always misses you."

KNOCK! KNOCK!

"Got dammit. WHAT?"

"Mazza, can we talk?" I heard just as Zia was about to sit on the toilet and do her thing.

"Beat it Tionne." I rested my head against the door and Zia winked at me. Her mouth opened and I anticipated the feeling she was about to give me.

"Pleaseeee! Mazza, I'm sorry." Zia scrunched her face up, stood and pulled my jeans up.

"Fuck her babe. Keep going."

"Mazza, you know how I get into it and if she's gonna keep interrupting I'm gonna be mad." I pulled her close and my dick damn near broke from how hard it was.

"Don't do me like that."

"I promise to do you even better later." She buckled my jeans and washed her hands. I opened the door, slid out of it and moved away. No one needed to know we were in there together.

"What up cousin Maz? Where my side piece at?" Shakim stood there with his arms folded.

"Side piece?"

"Yea. Ty is my main chick and Zia's my side piece."

"Boy, go somewhere." Tionne said and he ran off. I waited for her to speak and got ready for her long drawn out speech on why she did this or that.

I stood in front of my cousin trying to figure out what to say. I knew he was still mad and I don't blame him. I held a secret that could've cost him his life, all because I was trying to get her myself. It's unfortunate he found out on his own because it does look like I wasn't ever gonna mention it. I mean, I was; just not sure when.

"What?" He had an attitude and didn't appear to wanna be around me or hear anything I had to say. The only reason I did approach him is because of Shawn. He said, enough time went by for him to at least calm down.

"I'm sorry for not telling you about Riley."

"And?"

"And the moment I found out, it was my responsibility to let you know."

"That's it?"

"I don't know what else to say Mazza besides I was wrong. I let my hatred towards her get in the way and allowed you to spend multiple years with a woman who murdered your mentor and my kids father."

170

"Keep going." He circled his finger in the air as if he were waiting on me to say something else.

"I miss you and Fazza." He even stopped speaking to me. I expected it because they're close as hell but it was killing me not to have either of them checking up on me.

"Bye Tionne." He was about to walk away. I grabbed his elbow and he turned around.

"That's it?"

"What you want me to say Tionne?"

"How about I'm sorry Riley shot you or something. I took a bullet in the chest and.-"

"And that's your fault."

"My fault?"

"Yes, your fault. It never would've happened had you mentioned it because she'd be dead."

"You mean to tell me she's still alive even after hearing everything?" I was shocked they hadn't put her in the ground yet.

"Yes she is and you know why?"

"Why?"

"Because she disappeared knowing you'd tell the truth. I've been searching for that bitch high and low Tionne to make sure she gets exactly what she deserves." He backed me into a corner. I could see my mother and aunt on their way over. His girlfriend stood there not saying a word; not that I blame her.

"Your stupidity allowed her to get away."

"I know and I'm sorry."

"Sorry huh? Do you know she told Tariq who my girl was and that nigga stabbed her?" I covered my mouth because no one told me.

"Yea, Zia had to get over a hundred stitches in her arm and over fifty on her wrist all because Riley was mad. Then, she had me partly believing she was carrying my kid, knowing the entire time she told another man the same thing." I felt bad after listening to everything Riley did and has done.

"I find out she had something to do with killing Shakim and my own fucking cousin knew and didn't say shit. All of the bullshit we've gone through could've been avoided because she would've met her demise already. So before you come in my face telling me to basically get over it and move on; think about all the shit I had to endure first."

"That's enough Mazza." My mom pulled him back as the tears raced down my face. He was very angry and I knew we would never be close again.

"You ok?" My aunt asked.

"Yea." I wiped my face. He grabbed his girl's hand and turned around.

"You want me to forgive and you don't even have the got damn decency to apologize to my girl for tryna sneak her because she told you about yourself."

"WHAT?" My mom and aunt shouted at the same time.

"Oh, I forgot to tell y'all. Tionne attempted to fight Zia not too long ago."

"Because she said you were wrong?" My mom asked and I nodded my head.

"While she's pregnant Tionne?" My aunt chimed in.

"I was upset and.-"

"I don't care what the fuck you were going through. That woman is not only pregnant but is about to marry your cousin. Are you crazy?"

"Mommy."

"Don't mommy me. Ain't nobody about to have separate BBQ's and shit because you're the most hated. You better figure out a way to fix this shit and I mean it Tionne Chambers."

"I tried ma but…"

"I don't wanna hear it. I need a got damn drink." My mom stormed off.

"Zia, I'm..." She put her hand up to stop me.

"Save your tired ass apology for a fake bitch."

"Excuse me."

"You're only apologizing because everyone is digging in your ass." Mazza stood in front of her.

"I would've respected you more had it been done without an audience. I'm good on you Tionne." She told Mazza she was ready to go.

"And don't worry about us ever speaking in the future. Any functions we need to attend at the same time, keep your distance and I'll do the same. Oh, and don't make the mistake of coming for me again while I'm pregnant because Mazza and Fazza won't always be there to stop me."

"Mazza, let your woman know I'm not the one she wanna threaten." He ran up on me so fast no one could stop him if they wanted to.

"And cousin or not, I'm not the one to let you slick threaten my fiancé. Tionne, we both know I will rock your ass to sleep right here in front of all these people." He had the inside of his thumb and index finger under my chin as he squeezed my cheeks together.

"FAZZA! SHAWN!" I heard my aunt yelling. People were tryna pull my cousin off me but it wasn't working.

"Tha fuck you say now Tionne damn? Ain't nobody got time to be wrestling him off you." Fazza said as him and Shawn finally pried him off me.

"Go home Mazza. Zia, your food is in Tupperware in the fridge." My aunt said and she walked towards the kitchen as Fazza and Shawn dragged Mazza out the door.

****

"I'm not about to go into why you didn't tell because at this point, I don't care." My aunt said and poured herself a shot. After the fiasco with my cousin, Fazza kicked everyone out.

"I do wanna know why you don't like Zia?" She drank the vodka, made a face as it went down and slammed the glass on the mini bar.

"She's the one who brought Mazza over to ask about Riley when he was mad. Had she waited, he and I could've discussed it like adults."

"I should smack the shit outta your stupid ass." My mother said and took a shot with my aunt.

"First off... when either of the twins are angry, who in their right minds would try and stop them? And second... how you mad at her when you messed up?" I put my head down.

"Exactly! Then, instead of leaving it alone until Mazza was ready to talk, you bring it up again and threaten his girl."

176

"Ma, she said slick shit first."

"No she didn't. What she did say is, don't try and fight her again while she's pregnant because no one's gonna stop her from hitting you back." I looked at her.

"She had every right to let you know in case you tried it again. And when did you feel the need to start sneaking women? Girl, we raised you better than that." My aunt said.

"I was so mad and…"

"It's no excuse Tionne. What if she would've miscarried?"

"I didn't touch her. Shawn stopped me."

"Not the point Tionne. You doing dumb shit to conceal the foul crap you did. Now you're taking it out on a woman who had absolutely nothing to do with it. She didn't know Mazza was gonna act like that and from what Fazza told us before he left, had she not been there, he may have sent you to the hospital. Hell, the least you could do is thank her."

For the remainder of the time we were there, both of them continued to let me have it. I sat there and took it because they were right about it all. I was dead ass wrong in all aspects.

I guess, from here on out all I can do is hope Mazza speaks to me in the future because right now, I don't see it happening any time soon. Shawn came in not too long after and said he was ready to go. I kissed my mom and aunt on the cheek and headed out.

"I'm gonna stay at my place for a while." Shawn said when he helped me bring Shakima in. She had fallen asleep on the way home and Shakim went over Fazza's.

"Why?"

"Tionne, I love you to death but you keep bringing unnecessary drama in your life and I'm not sure I wanna be a part of it. I told you before your drama, is my drama but damn."

"What are you saying Shawn?" My eyes were glassy.

"We need a break."

"I don't want a break. Please don't leave me." He rested his forehead on mine.

"Call me when you're done with this petty and childish behavior." He pecked my lips and opened the front door.

"Please don't go."

"I love you Tionne. Don't make me wait forever." I dropped to my knees and cried hysterically when he closed the door. I really messed up this time.

Tyler

"Ty, where have you been?" I heard in a hush tone and turned around and came face to face with my mother. Today was my last day at work and I only came for the small baby shower they threw for me. I thought it was a regular party because I'll be out. It was cute and I appreciated the gesture. I do wanna know how the hell my mother knew I was here.

"What do you want?" I tried to get away from her because I know Fazza has someone watching me. It's no telling if today, would be the day he took her life and I don't wanna be around when it happens.

I know people may think I'm foul for allowing him to kill her but what am I supposed to do? She's harassed Fazza, belittled, had him arrested and accusing him of rape. How much do I expect him to take and how can I be ok with it? I can't. I love my mother to death and I wish things were different but they're not.

I've tried talking to Fazza and even threatened to leave but once my mother put him in a position to do jail time due to her lies, I washed my hands with the situation. It's only so much a person can take and he's had enough. I can understand her being upset about him shooting me, however; I moved on, why couldn't she? Or why didn't she stay away from him?

"Why are you treating me like this?" I stopped and turned around. I pushed her in a corner. It's no telling what would happen if she stepped out the building but then again, she had to come through the doors to get in.

"I'm not treating you like anything."

"Why haven't you answered my calls or come by to check on me?"

"Where am I seeing you at? The house is no longer there and..."

"Thanks to your loser ass baby daddy." She crossed her arms across her chest. I scoffed up a laugh.

"What did you expect him to do?"

"Wait a minute. You're ok with it?"

"No I'm not; just like I'm not ok with you falsely accusing him of rape." She rolled her eyes.

"What the hell were you thinking?" She rubbed the side of my arm.

"Ty, that man is very dangerous. Why are you lowering your standards?" I noticed she totally bypassed me asking why she accused him of rape.

"Who I decide to be with is my business."

"Ty, you're not thinking clearly."

"Ma, you're not thinking clearly. Do you have any fucking idea what you did? Huh?" I had to be careful with my words because I don't know if she had a wire or not.

"Don't speak to me that way. I'm still your mother."

"I'm speaking to you like this because you're not listening." I grabbed the top of her shoulders and forced her to look at me.

"You put me in a position to choose and it's not fair."

"What's not fair is you standing here telling me in so many words, you're choosing a man over your mother." I stepped back and wiped my eyes that were now allowing my tears to flow. How can a woman who birthed and raised me refuse to take responsibility for her own shit?

"Why don't you want me to be happy?"

"Excuse me!"

182

"I'm pregnant with twins and this is supposed to be a happy time for me. Instead, all I've been doing is stressing myself out because my mother wants to see my kids father locked up over her foolishness."

"Him shooting you, is not foolishness."

"MA, YOU ACCUSED HIM OF TRYING TO RAPE YOU. THEN, YOU CLAIMED TO BE SCARED FOR YOUR LIFE AND RUNNING AROUND TOWN MAKING UP STORIES!" I yelled in one breath. People were staring at us now.

"Sit down Ty." I heard and saw Mary rushing over to me.

"You ok?" She held my hand and told me to breathe.

"Where's your phone?" I handed it to her.

"Let me call Fazza."

"NOOO!" I shouted but it was too late. She walked away with the phone and I heard her telling him to get to the hospital.

"Ma, just go."

"I wanna stay here and make sure you're ok."

"Ma, please. I'll be ok." I know her fate is awaiting her but I don't want him doing anything in front of me. I also don't need her calling the cops and accusing him of nonsense again. I felt my stomach knotting up and tried my hardest to calm down.

"He will not force me to…"

"Mrs. Evans, if she's asking you to go, please exit the building." Mary said and handed me my phone.

"I don't have to go anywhere. This is a public hospital."

"Security. Escort this woman out please. She's causing discomfort and stress to one of our employees."

"I am not leaving. My daughter is under distress and I'm staying to make sure she's ok." It felt like my head was spinning and I can't tell you what happened because once again, I passed out.

****

"Fazza, calm down. She's ok." I heard Zia's voice as I opened my eyes.

"Honey, you being this upset, is only going to upset her." I glanced around the room and saw Ms. Chambers, Mary, Zia, Mazza, Kelly and his girlfriend.

184

"Is she ok?" The reverend stepped in asking.

"I'm ok." I sat up slow. Fazza rushed to my side and ran his hand down my face. I could see love, sadness and most of all anger. I give him credit for trying to cover it up but it wasn't working.

"Are my babies ok?" He smiled.

"Our babies are fine."

"I love you Fazza." I started crying and he asked everyone to give us a minute.

"I know you don't wanna hear this but she wanted you to lose the babies."

"What?"

"When you passed out, she told everyone to leave you alone. She is your next of kin and unfortunately, they didn't know what to do."

"How did I get here?"

"Mary said, she had security literally drag her out and made them bring you up here." Tears flooded my face as he finished describing the fiasco my mother caused downstairs.

Did she hate me so much, she wished death on my children? Why didn't she just leave when I told her to?

"Why is she doing this to me?"

"It's not you Ty; it's me. She wants me away from you and if you have my kids, she knows I ain't going nowhere."

"Fazza, I'm so sorry she's doing all this. Your life was fine before me and now she is tryna hurt you. Baby, maybe I should just leave..." He shushed me with his finger.

"You're not going anywhere Ty. Her actions aren't a depiction of you and won't change my feelings."

"But..."

"But nothing. We're never breaking up so don't bring it up again." He kissed me passionately and had me lay back on the pillow.

"How are you feeling?" He asked. I told him I needed the bathroom and removed the plugs from the machine to get up.

"I'm ok." He helped me out the bed to clean myself up. After I got back in, he sat next to me and I could tell something was on his mind.

"I tried to leave her alone Ty, I swear but this is gone on long enough. Its time." I nodded my head and hugged him. I didn't say anything because he's right. Fazza, could have terminated my mother a long time ago.

"Alright, y'all had enough time. We coming back in. Are you ok sweetie?" Ms. Chambers asked and Fazza wiped my tears.

"Nephew, I know you weren't in here trying to beat her coochie up." I almost choked listening to him.

"Yo, how are you even still a reverend with your perverted ass?"

"One... I wasn't always saved and two... have you seen the way those church women come to church these days? Hell, their dresses are painted on and the way their butts and tities bust out is inappropriate but who am I to tell them not to dress the way they want?" He had a devious grin on his face.

"You nasty unc." Zia had her mouth covered laughing.

"Why you think I be having sex with my wife in my office? Shoot, my man down below definitely be hard looking

187

at them. Thank goodness for those oversized robes, otherwise the congregation would see a lot."

"Ok, that's enough." Ms. Chambers said.

"I'm not ever going to his church." Zia said and Mazza busted out laughing.

"Girl, ain't nobody looking at you. Now if you and my nephew ever break up, that's a different story. I'm gonna look and..." He wiped that smile right off Mazza face.

"Boy, ain't nobody scared of you. Now Zia, like I was saying...-" He tried to sit next to her and Mazza stood in front of him. I have to admit it was funny and definitely brought me outta the slump I was in for the moment.

"I love you Ty." He laid back on the bed with me.

"Don't worry about your mother anymore." I snapped my neck to look at him.

"I won't give you any information but set up the services. Do you want my uncle to do the eulogy or anything?" We both looked at Mazza grilling his uncle and everyone else laughing.

"I'm not sure she even deserves one after this but let me think on it." He kissed my forehead, placed his hand in mine and stayed next to me, laughing and joking with everyone else. I said a silent prayer to God asking him to forgive my mother for her sins and if he had to send her to hell, it is, what it is.

"Yo unc, keep fucking with me and see what happens."
I told him as we were walking out Ty's room. They were
keeping her overnight to make sure she didn't dilate. They
wanted my niece and nephew to stay inside for as long as
possible.

When Fazza received the call from Mary, we were on
our way to Maryland to get Riley. I turned the car around fast
as hell and raced to the hospital. The way Mary described the
shit going down at the hospital, you would think Ty's mother
wanted her and the kids to die. Who tells the hospital staff not
to care for a woman who passed out?

She even had the nerve to throw in there, she's her
only kin and they had to do what she said. Mary did mention at
first, they were stuck but then told her mother they can't deny
her medical care and threw her out.

My brother was bugging after hearing she had dilated
two centimeters and could possibly go into early labor. Kelly
and I both knew what he was ready to do and neither of us said
a word.

Once we got to the hospital, the word was put out about Ty's mom. At this point, Ty had to come to grips that her mother would no longer be around. Fazza, has been doing a lotta funny shit to her and could've killed her at any time but didn't. I think he was trying his hardest not to hurt Ty, by getting rid of her but it's no way he's allowing her to slide and I didn't blame him.

"Mazza, you can't curse at the reverend." Zia said as she held my hand. My uncle had the nerve to grin.

"Why not?"

"Baby, we don't need any bad luck."

"Yea, nephew. You know God and I have a good relationship." He smirked.

"Maybe, you and the devil because God ain't fucking with you." Zia smacked me on the arm and pushed me off the elevator.

"Let me talk to you real quick nephew."

"Umm, should I stand here?" I looked at my uncle and he gave me a look that told me to let her sit in the car.

"Nah babe. You need to sit anyway." She pecked my lips and opened the car door. I went on the other side to start it and turned the radio up a little. My uncle and I moved to the back of to speak.

"I already know what's about to happen with Ty's mother but I also want you to be careful going to Maryland." I didn't even ask how he knew because I'm sure my mother had no problem running her mouth. The three of them were very tight so I know he'll bring up the shit with Tionne as well.

"I will."

"Good and this mess with Tionne has your mom and aunt getting on my nerves. Tell me real quick what went down." I gave him the short version because I didn't want Zia sitting in the car too long.

"That's what Tionne gets. I told my sister she needed to stop babying her a long time ago."

"What you mean?"

"Tionne is the only girl out of all the kids." He had two boys as well but both of them were doing their own thing. One was in New York and the other in California. They definitely didn't live the way we did but we spoke to them all the time.

"She was dead wrong and took it out on your woman. I bet she thought you'd take her side and when you didn't, she had a fit. Therefore; she won't approve of Zia now because she feels it's her fault."

"I get it and had she not come for Zia, we would've probably moved past it. But how you try and attack a pregnant woman?" My uncle was shaking his head.

"That's where she fucked up and then to slick threaten her at the house only verified how petty she was. Say what you want but Tionne fucked us up; not Zia, not Riley, not anyone but her."

"I agree but you know women see things the way they want."

"I know but Tionne ain't stupid and she knows better."

"Listen, Zia is your fiancé and Tionne is your cousin. I get you don't wanna mess with her anymore but make sure it doesn't trickle down on the kids. Those kids look to you and Fazza as their father figure." I nodded and told them I'd never do that. He and I finished speaking for a few more minutes and as he was about to leave he turned around.

"Oh yea, Shawn left her ass too."

"Word!"

"Yup. He told her she was bringing too much unnecessary drama and she had to get her life together."

"Good for him."

"That's what I said." He walked to his car. My uncle may be ghetto as hell but he's no fool when it comes to family.

"Everything ok?"

"Yea, we good. You hungry?" She gave me a death stare.

"What? I have to make sure you and my baby eats."

"Whatever but since you asked, I can go for some Burger King." I had to laugh at her. Always talking about she ain't hungry but when you mention food, she jumps right on it.

****

"Don't say shit to Bridget when you go inside." I told my brother when we stopped at the same Dunkin Donuts I met Zia at. Ty was home with my mother, resting peacefully. Fazza

194

even made her turn the phone off so her mom couldn't contact her. She wouldn't at this point anyway but he wanted her to feel like she was ok, I guess.

"Man, be quiet."

"Hurry up."

"You not coming in?" He asked and both me and Kelly gave him a hell no look.

"What?"

"Nigga, don't nobody wanna smell your ass or hear about you clogging the toilet." He reached in his pocket and pulled some bottle out.

"Goes to show how much you know. My girl brought me this for when I travel."

"What the hell is that?" Kelly snatched it out his hand.

"V.I.Poo. What's this?" Fazza snatched it back.

"For your information it's to keep the smell away as I'm going." Zia told me Ty was gonna buy it at the store but Shanta came in and they left. She must've went back to get it. I don't blame her because my brother definitely stinks when he goes.

"Yea your girl is special too."

"Fuck you nigga." He went to walk inside.

"Wait!" I said and stood outside the car.

"What?" He had the door open to go in.

"Does it stop you from clogging the toilet too?" I was being funny.

"Hell no. They beat for that."

"You shot the hell out." Kelly shouted.

"And my shit isn't gonna be runny, so Bridget better call the plumber soon as I walk in." He shrugged his shoulders and went in. We couldn't stop laughing.

"What's up sexy?" I answered when Zia called.

"I miss you and I'm horny." I snapped my neck to look at Kelly because my blue tooth was on. He was shaking his head laughing. I took her off and got out the car to talk in private.

"Babe, you know my phone goes to Bluetooth."

"I'm sorry but who cares? I'll be delivering soon and won't be able to get any right away. Have phone sex with me."

"Zia, really?" She didn't respond, hung up and facetime'd me. She was naked on her knees and playing with her pussy from behind.

"You don't play fair."

"Nope. Mmmmm Mazza. I miss your tongue sliding in and out my pussy. Ssssss, I wanna suck your dick until you cum in my mouth." My dick was rising by the second. I had to hang up on her, otherwise; I'd pull my shit out and continue with her. She tried to FaceTime me back but I refused to answer. I sent her a text telling her, I'd see her when I got home and she better have that same energy.

"She got yo dick hard huh?" Fazza said coming out the store. I was adjusting myself the best I could.

"Whatever."

"Did you clog the toilet?" Kelly asked from the back seat.

"Yup. Let's go." He said it with no problem. I'd hate to be the person to clean up after him.

On the ride to get Riley, my mind was all over the place. Here was a woman I was madly in love with at one time, about

197

to lose her life for lying, and killing Shakim. I was pissed about her cheating too but not as much. I had my little head shots here and there from bitches at work, but they never got me to fuck them. Right or wrong, Riley was fucking, sucking and now having a baby by someone else.

It's been a few times, I thought of not taking her life, then I'd think about what Zia said to my cousin and get mad again. At any time, Riley could've killed me in my sleep, or murdered me the same exact way she got Shakim. Not once did Tionne mention it and that bothers the fuck outta me too. She had plenty of times to come clean; regardless of hearing how in love we were.

Tionne was selfish as hell and had the nerve to try and take it out on my girl, or should I say tried because Zia wasn't playing any games with her. The only reason I snapped on Tionne when she slick threatened her, is because no matter how good of a fighter Zia may be, my cousin has deadly hands, thanks to us. I'd never let them fight but still, it's the point. Why did she even come for Zia in the first place because she was wrong? I was over it and Tionne better hope in the future we can move past it but as of right now I don't see it happening.

We pulled up to the country looking house Riley was staying in. Not that I wouldn't have found her, but the dumb bitch never changed her phone number, therefore; our tech guy tracked her with no problem.

I would've thought she'd leave being we were caught up at the hospital with my brother and Ty, but nope. She thinks living out here in this spot is gonna save her. Jordan did run into Zia's mom and begged her to ask if I could wait until Riley delivered the baby to kill her. I don't think I could do it.

"You good bro?" Fazza asked as I sat there in the black SUV staring at the house.

"Yea. Just tryna wrap my head around the shit."

"I'll do it, if you can't."

"It has to be me."

"Why is that? Shit, Shakim was my mentor too."

"Yea, but I'm the one she lived with. The one, she held it from and kept living her life as if she didn't. Six long years of knowing the truth and never slipped up once. Yea, it has to be me." The thought of it, made me upset all over again.

We got out and I walked down to one of the others. We came six trucks deep in case some shit kicked off. People can think because its Riley we didn't need as many people but you never know with her. Shit, we already knew she had two bodyguards, so it's no telling what she had going on.

"Stay in this fucking truck. If you get out, your dead on sight." He nodded his head with fear on his face.

"You!" I pointed to the other guy and told him to get his shit and come on.

It was after nine and the sun had gone down by now. There were a few cars riding by but nothing outta the ordinary, which is a good thing because we didn't need anyone being nosy and contacting the police.

We now had the house surrounded and I was at the front door. I thought about knocking but what for?

BOOM! I shot the lock off and nothing. There was no screaming or anyone to even attempt to shoot. I heard music upstairs and took my time going up. I felt a presence behind me and didn't have to look, to know my brother was right there and I'm sure Kelly, behind him. We got to the door and opened it, only to find this bitch getting fucked from the back and sucking another guys dick. Her stomach was out there too.

"I guess old habits die hard." I shot the guy fucking her, in the head and his body dropped to the ground instantly. Fazza, caught the other dude in the forehead. Lucky for him, he was already lying down so his body didn't drop. Riley's was frozen with fear. I nodded my head and both Fazza and Kelly walked out.

"Why, Riley?" She pretended not to know what I was speaking of.

"Why would you kill Shakim? Why would you stay with me all those years?" I should've killed her on the spot but I had to know. The tears raced down her face.

"I was in love with him Mazza and he treated me like shit."

"You didn't have to kill him."

"I was young and he hurt me bad."

"You didn't have to kill him." I said again.

"Then you start fucking with me, knowing how close we were and never said a word."

"I swear, I didn't know at first. Shit, I just recently found out Tionne was your cousin. He kept me away from my own family, I had no friends and the list goes on and on."

"YOU DIDN'T HAVE TO KILL HIM RILEY!" I shouted and stood up. She backed up and fell on top of one of the guys.

"Faz, bring dude up here." I went to help her up, gripped the side of her arm and took her in another room.

"Oh, you were really getting ready huh?" I glanced around the room and there was a crib, stroller and mad baby shit.

"Mazza, please don't kill me."

"All you had to do was tell me Riley. I'm not saying we would've stayed together but you wouldn't be about to go through this." I nodded for the guy to come in and set up. We brought Mary with us because Ty couldn't come.

At first, I was nervous about her but Ty told me she could be trusted, especially; since we paid her and Fazza threatened her life. She was so damn scared, she almost didn't come. Ty, had to make Fazza promise not to touch her in order for her to agree.

"What's going on?" Mary wasted no time shooting her in the arm with a syringe to sedate her. I think she was tryna hurry up and go back home.

"Then, you sent Tariq to try and kill my fiancé." Her eyes grew really big.

"Fiancé?" She questioned now slurring at her words.

"Yup and she's about to have my first child." Her body was becoming weaker by the second.

"Mazza, you never gave me a baby or even proposed."

"Everything happens for a reason Riley." I pushed her down on the bed and watched as the medical doctor performed a C-section on her.

The night Zia's mom called to tell me Jordan begged and kept asking, if she could get me not to kill Riley until she delivered, I spoke to Zia about it. I don't usually murder kids and since it was still in her stomach, I didn't look at it that way. Zia told me that even though Jordan is a dick, he shouldn't have to suffer by losing a child because of the things Riley did. She asked, how I would feel if the roles were reversed and I admit it had me thinking.

I drove to Maryland alone the next day, met up with Jordan, beat his ass again and told him if he ever spoke a word of this to anyone, he'd be dead, as well as his kids and the rest of his family.

Once he agreed, I spoke to my boy Cason who dealt with a similar situation and this is the advice he gave. *Find the bitch, take the baby out her stomach and kill her instantly, that way you won't have time to feel bad or have time to change your mind.* And this is exactly what happened, using the same medical doctor he did.

He told me, this guy was very sanitary and had people who worked at hospitals along the East Coast who won't question a thing when he brought the child in. I appreciated the hell outta him because had I not listened, Riley and this little girl would be dead.

I stood there watching the baby being removed from her stomach and placed in a small crib like thing. The doctor and Mary removed their gloves, placed them in the black garbage bag we had to remove any evidence and ran out with the child, who I couldn't even tell if she was alive or not. I walked over to Riley who was still awake, crying but couldn't move. Stomach wide open, blood gushing out and all.

"Tell your parents, I said what's up bitch."

POW! POW! There was no silencer and the sound only verified for me she was dead and gone. I didn't bother to close her eyes or cover her up.

"Let's go. They already started to put gasoline around the house and you know it'll explode two minutes after." My brother pushed me out the room.

"Where is he?" I asked about Jordan who was in the truck waiting. Fazza pointed and he was getting out with two suitcases.

"It's all there." He handed them to me and I opened one up to see the money stacked neatly.

"Tell Zia, I'm sorry for everything and thanks again for allowing my daughter to live." I noticed a tear fall down his face.

"Believe it or not, Zia is the one who saved her."

"Zia?"

"Yup because I could care less about what happened to the kid." I closed the suitcase and walked up on him.

"You know, even though you treated Zia like a piece of shit, stole her money out her account, had two babies on her and constantly harassed her; she still made sure you didn't suffer." He put his head down.

"Thank you for fucking up, because you placed a beautiful woman in my life." He didn't say anything.

"No need to thank her either."

"Huh?"

"You don't have to call, text, email or anything to thank her. Trust me, she'll get all the thanks she needs from me." I hit him with the peace sign and we pulled off after watching the house explode.

The ride to Delaware seemed short because one minute, I'm asleep and the next, Fazza is pulling up in my driveway. I guess that's what happens when you're at peace.

Zia opened the door and smiled. I was deeply in love with her and couldn't wait until we exchanged vows and had our child.

"Tell your girl not to call Ty for a few days because I need to fuck as much as I can before my kids come." I busted out laughing, grabbed the money out the back and went inside the house.

"I missed you." She wrapped her hands around my neck.

"You have to get in the shower babe." She let go and followed me upstairs. I sat the suitcases on the bed and told her to look in it. I stripped, went in the bathroom to shower and scrubbed myself down. I came out and saw her sitting on the bed with a confused look.

"Mazza, why do you have all this money?"

"It's yours."

"Mine? Why would you bring me this money?" I smiled and sat next to her with my towel still wrapped around my waist.

"This is the money Jordan stole from your bank account, plus interest."

"Oh my God! Wait! This looks like more than 55k." I pecked her lips and went to grab me some boxers to put on.

"Its four million dollars." I knew his ass was rich and made sure he gave her what I thought was necessary. I would've asked for more but she had me, so money would never be an object anyway.

"WHATTTTT?"

"Is that not enough?"

"That's way too much." I put my boxers on and grabbed the lotion.

"I told him it was for all the pain and suffering you went through. The mental and verbal abuse. The time he backed you into the wall and bruised your tailbone and all the embarrassment you had to deal with too." She started crying.

"Do you want more because I'm sure he'll have no problem giving it to you?" That nigga was scared to death of me and whatever I asked for, I'm sure he'd do it with no questions asked.

"No. How did you? Why did you?"

"You deserve it baby." She pushed it off the bed and maneuvered herself on my lap.

"I love you so much." She cried and laid her head on my shoulder.

"Zia, there's mothing I won't do for you. All I ask, is you stay faithful and if ever you feel something's wrong, you talk to me about it." She nodded and stood.

"I'm never leaving you." She smiled and made sure to remind me of one reason, I'll never leave. My ass was sleep right after.

"Fazza, where are we?" Ty asked when we pulled up to the new house. I didn't wanna bring her here until after our kids were born. This was supposed to be her push gift but it looks like I have to find something else now.

When we returned from Maryland it was late but my mom was still up. She told me, it's probably better to get her outta the old house because its where her mom used to visit at one point and may have had bad memories. I moved all her shit into storage so if she wants to go through it, she could.

"Our new house." She turned to look at me with a huge grin on her face.

"You were listening."

"Technically, this house was already in the process of being purchased but I do listen."

"Why couldn't you give me my moment? Let me think I had an influence on you being nice." She opened the door and I put my hand on her arm to stop her.

"You have a huge influence on me Ty, whether you see it or not."

"I do."

"Yea. I've calmed down a lot due to you being in my life."

"Well good. That lesson I taught you was serious." I sucked my teeth.

"Now who being petty?"

"Me." She raised her little hand being smart.

"Get out." We closed the door to her truck and walked around the front looking at the landscaping.

"Nice. Can we go inside?" I handed her the keys and watched as her eyes lit up the second she opened the door.

I had Zia ask her on many occasions what she liked as far as furniture and the things she wanted in her new house. I made sure to purchase everything. The babies room were done as well but if she wanted to change it, I had no problem with it.

"How many bedrooms?" I helped her up the steps.

"Seven."

"Why so many?"

"Shit, I already put two babies in you the first round. There's no telling how many I'll put in each time I get you pregnant."

"You bugging Fazza. These two will be enough for now." She patted her belly.

"Like I said, for all the kids I put in you, I wanted to make sure we had the space. If not, we can add on as well." She waved me off and checked each room. When she finished we went in the master bedroom.

"Too bad you have to wait to try this bed out." She sat back and gapped her legs open. Even though she wore leggings I could still see her pussy print and grabbed my dick.

"Or I could have another..." I felt a pillow go upside my head.

"Don't play with me Fazza."

"I'm just saying." She told me to come closer and made me get on my knees.

"You ain't saying shit. Take what you want and be gentle." I stripped both of us outta our clothes and entered my safe haven.

By the time we finished, it was late and I had things to do. I ordered some food, waited for it to come and made sure she was comfortable before leaving.

"Be safe baby." I leaned down and kissed her lips.

"Always. I'll lock up and don't go downstairs." Her stomach was huge and I know it was hard to climb the steps. I didn't want her to fall an no one is there to help.

"I'm going to sleep anyway." I walked out the room and out the house.

"You ready?" Kelly asked and passed me the blunt. He was waiting in the car.

"It's time to get this over with."

"Mazza's already there waiting." I nodded and put my seatbelt on. This nigga drives crazy and I'll be damned if he kills me before handling this.

****

I stood in my office at Chambers place watching this bitch squirm, cry, bitch, complain and whine in the chair. It took me a very long time to get here and I tried my hardest to stall but after this last stunt, it's no more waiting. She had to go and it had to be today.

See, the day she went to the hospital, I already knew her whereabouts because my girl was there. I had no idea she almost forced Ty to go into early labor so when Mary contacted me, all I saw was red.

Mazza couldn't get there fast enough and when he did, my mind was on Ty. It doesn't mean my brother didn't handle shit for me, which is why this bitch is about to meet her demise. I picked my phone up and called my fiancé. I had to hear her voice before the deed was done.

"Yea babe." She sounded asleep.

"Ty, promise you won't leave after it's done."

"After what's done Fazza? Are you ok?" I could hear worry in her voice.

"Promise you won't leave." I loved the hell outta her and if she tried to leave because of what I'm about to do, I would never forgive myself for having to keep her locked away. I meant what I said about us never breaking up but I do like to make her think she can.

214

"Fazza, I trust you to do what needs to be done to protect your family and that includes me. I won't ever leave you for that."

"Say no more. Go back to sleep."

"Fazza?"

"Yea." I went to open the door of the office.

"I love you and don't have any second thoughts. Whatever it is you're about to do, do it with confidence and no regrets."

"I love you too Ty and I'll be home soon."

"Good, because I need to feel you next to me." I smiled at her last statement. She tells me all the time she can sleep but it's not a good one, unless I'm next to her.

I placed my phone in the clip and pressed the elevator to go downstairs. Music was blasting as the door opened. Maz and Kelly were in there drinking and playing the video game. A few other guys were sitting at the other table talking.

I stepped closer to Ty's mother and stopped directly in front of her. She lifted her head and peed on herself. I loved the affect I had on her shit talking ass. I grabbed a chair and sat down.

"Why don't you like me Ms. Evans?" I lit a blunt and blew smoke in her face.

"You don't respect my daughter and she deserves better."

"Says the woman who tried to make her go into early labor."

"Did she have them?"

"No and if you're wondering, she's doing fine in her new house." She sucked her teeth.

"I'm not gonna sit here and have a heart to heart because I see you're the type of woman who is old and set in her ways. I do wanna say one thing before I snatch your life from your body."

"Please don't."

"Wow, you're begging?" I smirked and looked over at my brother who was shaking his head.

"They always do at the last minute." Kelly shouted over the music.

"I was gonna torture you by placing you against the wall and throw darts at you." The darts had titanium tips like the bow and arrows, which mean they would pierced every spot I hit.

"Instead, I brought someone else to do it. That way, I won't feel bad for murdering my kids grandmother."

"Ty, won't kill me." She smiled assuming her daughter would be the one who did it,

"What up nephew?" My uncle stepped in with his wife who had a hateful look on her face.

"What up?" His wife walked straight passed me and started beating the crap outta Ms. Evans.

"This will teach your ass to sleep with a married man." She shouted and continued whooping her ass.

My family never cared for her but my uncle loved her and if he was still rocking with her, so were we. Plus, I still call her my aunt and she's the mother to my two cousins so it's only fair to give her this moment.

To my knowledge, my uncle never cheated once they got married. He only got caught because Ty's mother became a stalker after fucking my uncle. *Yea, good dick run in this family.*

She was calling nonstop, pretending to discuss church things. She sent nasty text messages and other shit. His wife found out and put him in the doghouse, the same way Ty did me.

My uncle was livid and the day Ty got out the hospital, he called and said his wife wanted to kill her. What better way for me not to feel as guilty and let her do it. Yea, I'm still the one who had her killed but at least, it won't be by my hands.

"Where is it?" My aunt asked and I handed her the shot gun she requested. I asked why she chose that and she looked at my uncle.

"I'ma put a hole in her heart, the same way she did mine when I found out my husband cheated on me." My uncle put his head down.

"Please don't. I'm sorry. We were both going through something and..."

BOOM! Her body hit the ground and she smiled.

"If you ever stick your dick in another woman, I'm gonna do you the same way." She handed me the gun and kissed my uncle on the cheek.

"I say, you do it now." Mazza was laughing and tryna egg her on.

"Nephew, I'm gonna make sure God denies your entrance to heaven."

"Whatever." My aunt came over to where Mazza and I stood.

"We may not be close and I know your mom and aunt can't stand me." She smirked.

"The feelings are mutual but it doesn't mean I don't love you two." She kissed our cheeks and went to leave.

"I want an invitation to the wedding, baby shower, and whatever else you two have. We're family and whether we get along or not, I won't ever turn my back on any of you. Let's go nigga." My uncle didn't say a word and hurried behind her.

"What now?" Kelly asked.

"What you mean?"

"Well, all the bad characters in our story are dead, we need to make new enemies." We all busted out laughing.

"Nah. You know Tina J don't go past 3 books in a series. I'm sure the new one will be just as good but no one will ever be better than Fazza Chambers." Everyone shook their heads and walked out the door. Say what you want but my character was the **SHIT!!!!!**

One year later....

"Yo, nephew. Where is your fiancé?" My uncle asked in the church as we stood there waiting on Ty, to grace us with her presence. It's been a long time coming but today is my wedding day.

"Man, I don't know. You know we black and on CP time."

"Well, she better hurry up."

"Why?"

"Nephew, I know you see these women and the tight ass dresses they have on. This robe is covering me now but my thang ain't little so it's bound to poke out."

"Yo, I need a new reverend right now."

"What? The podium is usual in in front of me." He shrugged his shoulders and I could hear Mazza cracking up.

"That's exactly why Zia and I exchanged vows in Bermuda."

"I'm started to think, we should've done the same thing." Three months after Zia gave birth to my niece Mazie, the doctor said it was ok for them to fly. She set the wedding up for the next month and they had a destination wedding. It was nice as hell and believe it or not, pretty crowded. People loved Zia in Maryland and did everything to make it to her wedding. Then, our family showed up as well. We had a good time.

Ty, initially wanted to have a double wedding but I told her ass, hell no. Shit, we were twins and did everything together all our life. We needed our own moment. Plus, I had to show off my banging ass tux and get all the attention.

The music started and the doors opened. In walked the wedding party and then Zia. I turned to look at my brother and he was mesmerized. Those two were extra sometimes with their shit and I couldn't stand to be around.

Zia told me I needed to stop pretending Ty doesn't have me the same and she's right, I just didn't show it out in the open a lot because then I'd wanna fuck. Ty, had that effect on me and we both knew it.

Once the doors closed again, I knew it was time. I fixed my cuffs and waited for my future wife to come down the aisle.

Beautiful wasn't the way to describe her because she was way beyond that. Each time she took a step, my heart started beating faster. This woman is the only one who could get me to settle down. She is my match and I wasn't gonna do anything to mess us up.

"You're gorgeous." I said, lifted her veil and placed a kiss on her lips.

"And you're handsome too." I wiped the tears in her eyes.

"Let's get this wedding started." My uncle said and we both turned to look at him. After saying a few words, he asked if we wanted to say our own vows. I was cool with the one's from the church but Ty said we had to. She said, because I'm so mean she wanted to hear how I really felt deep inside.

"Ladies first." She passed her bouquet to Zia and turned back to me.

"Fazza Chambers, I could start off speaking about how arrogant and ignorant you are but there's no need. Everyone in here knows the type of person you are on the outside but I'm the only one who knows you inside and out."

"Oh yea." I stood in a stance with my arms folded, waiting to hear what she thought she knew.

"Yup and let me tell you." She moved my arms and placed her hand on the side of my face.

"Fazza, when we met, I didn't think we'd ever get this far. You were blunt and very aggressive asking for my number and to this day, I'll never regret giving it to you. In two years, you are the only man who has my heart and I'm ready and willing to give you all of me. I feel like the time is right for our love to keep blossoming into being even more perfect." Damn, she was laying it on thick.

"Every day I wake up to you, I feel like one of those girls in the movie who met her prince. The way you smile, the way you kiss, the way you touch and the way you love me. You try your hardest to make sure I'm never in pain, even in the worst situations we've encountered." She took my hand in hers.

"Baby, I already know, I'll never leave because you're the man God placed in my life. We have two beautiful children who adore you, the same as I. Fazza Chambers as long as I breathe, you will never be alone and I will love you endlessly until I can't any longer. You are my prince charming, my king and my everything. I love you so much baby and I pray that we live a very long life just so I can say, I love you over and over." She wiped the few tears that left my eyes. Hell yea, I shed some tears. Her shit was deep as hell. I've never had a woman say anything like that to me.

"Your turn." I nodded and lifted Ty's face to look at me.

"Tyler Evans, you are the love of my life and everything a man could ever need. You may think I'm a dick, asshole and anything else you call me, but one thing you can't call me is a loser. I play tough but you can always depend on me."

"Babe, you can't curse in church." She tried to whisper.

"Please. Unc, does it all the time." I heard a few people laughing.

"Anyway, I may not say it a lot but I appreciate you being in my life, carrying my kids and making sure I'm good no matter what. You go hard for no reason at all sometimes, but I know it's because you want what's best for me. I'm here to let you know nothing will ever stand in the way of me loving you."

"Fazza." She tried to wipe the tears coming down her face but they kept falling.

"I know you love me and I love you so much more than words will ever say. I love every inch of you, from the top of your head to your feet and that ugly ass face you make when you cry." She smacked me on the arm.

"When you left me, I was mad at myself for hurting you and gave you your space but each day, I prayed for you to take me back. When you did, a nigga was happy like a pig in shit. I need you Ty and I'll never let you go." She smiled.

"And now look. We're writing history and they'll be talking about us twenty years from now and you know why. It's because no one thought I'd ever meet a woman who could tame me but you proved them all wrong." I took her hand in mine and kissed the top of them.

"Ty, I'll never hurt you again and I'm sorry for causing you pain. I'm giving you my word to love you to the end and no matter what, I'm gonna always be here. I could never walk away because no one can take your place and if it's not you and me, then I don't want anyone else. I love you Ty and I'm glad, I made you say yes." Everyone busted out laughing but she was hysterical crying.

"My vows were the shit, right?" I whispered in her ear and placed my lips on hers. We engaged in a very passionate kiss until we were pulled apart.

"Can we finish now?" My uncle asked and I nodded my head yes.

"I now pronounce you husband and wife. Everyone help me welcome, Mr. and Mrs. Fazza Chambers." People were clapping, snapping photos and hugging us. I ended up taking my daughter from my mom because she kept screaming for me. I know, I didn't want a little girl and this is why. She spoiled as fuck. I can't do shit without her being attached to my hip. My niece even had the nerve to be the same when she came to the house. My son was attached to the women, which I can expect. Like father, like son.

Anyway, Mazza and Zia are expecting their first set of twins in seven months. Zia, made them take a few ultrasounds to make sure it was twins. She was mad as hell but I don't know why. Shit, her husband is one. Ty and I just started working on our next baby and trust, I'm squirting in it every chance I get.

If you're wondering, no, Mazza and I still didn't fuck with Tionne. She did some foul shit and some things you can forgive and others you can't. For Mazza, she should've never gone after Zia and threatened her. For me, I just couldn't get over her holding in the secret and if she came for Zia, I had no doubt she'd try Ty and I'm not having it. So to avoid it, we stayed away. We still get Shakim's nasty ass and Shakima loves being around Ty and Zia.

Shawn took her back after my mom said she promised him, to do better and whatever else he left her for. At family functions, we don't speak and neither of us invited her to our

weddings or attended hers. Oh well, shit happens. **PEACE!**

Made in United States
Orlando, FL
20 February 2022

14986789R00127